Little One

Copyright © 2024 by Rachel O'Rourke

Little One published by Rachel O'Rourke

Text and illustration copyright, Rachel O'Rourke, 2024.

All rights reserved. No part of this publication may be reproduced or transmitted in any form or by any means, electronic or mechanical, including photocopying, recording, storage, in an information retrieval system, or otherwise, without prior written permission of the publisher, unless specifically permitted under the Australian Copyright Act 1968 as amended.

This book is a work of fiction. Names, characters, places, and incidents either are products of the author's imagination or are used fictitiously. Any resemblance to actual persons, living or dead, events, or locales is entirely coincidental.

Cover design by Alise Kisel

Images in this book are copyright-approved.

Illustrations within this book are copyright-approved.

Line and copy editing by Hummingbird Editing

Paperback ISBN: 9780975669440

eBook ISBN: 9780975669457

More great titles by Rachel O'Rourke can be found at

www.rachelorourke.com.au

LITTLE ONE

Content Warning

For further information, please scan the QR code for a list of possible content triggers.

By reading further, you, as the reader, are continuing with the understanding that not all possible triggers may have been mentioned. The author and any who contributed to this work cannot and will not be held accountable for a reader's actions, reactions, or state of mind after reading this book.

Little One

Daddy wants you to sit back, relax and treat yourself to some you time. Open this book and let the words take you away from all your responsibility.

Mmm, that's right. Daddy loves the way you look when immersed in a book.

Chapter 1

The Encounter

RACHEL O'ROURKE

Damon has been visiting the same BDSM club at least once a week for the last two years. He has been to many before this one, but something about the dimly lit red lights, the private back rooms, and the array of men that walk through the front door makes this one his favourite. What happens during each visit can change depending on the day he's had. After a long day analysing his business dealings, he could order a drink and enjoy his surroundings, or sit back and watch while others play. Damon especially loves to study people. To try to understand what they need and desire based on their behaviour and requests during a scene.

Of course, when the mood strikes, or if he has someone in his life, whether a boy toy, a submissive or a partner, he may also partake in a scene or two, whether public or in a private back room. That's always a discussion he has prior to playing.

However, for Damon, relationships seem to come and go. The longest he's had since the age of eighteen—when he began to date, even if they were much older men or sometimes married—was eighteen months. He thought he had found someone who understood his desires until that someone found another who was younger. Someone who played in the BDSM lifestyle but didn't live it twenty-four-seven. That relationship ended a year ago, and to Damon's surprise, it didn't upset him as much as it should have. He's thirty-five, yet hasn't been able to find the right person to satisfy his needs physically, mentally and sexually.

He prides himself on being a Dom Daddy. Over the years, his relationships have varied from being a full-time Daddy to simply stepping into that role during a scene. He's a Dominant, and a top, who needs to be challenged from time to time, and he thinks he's finally found that someone.

For two months, Damon has had his eye on a younger raven-haired boy who comes into the club well into the a.m. once a week, normally a Thursday, sometimes a Sunday. And yes, Damon has been making sure to be in the club both days, so he doesn't miss laying eyes on his new fascination.

The boy always walks into the club looking frustrated, biting his lip as his hazel eyes scan the room, hunting down his prey. He isn't afraid of public play, but it's never sexual. He always walks up to the biggest man in the room, and Damon watches as the younger boy bends over, taking the pounding of a paddle or a flog, his ghostly pale ass turning a sweet rose shade.

After five minutes, Damon's hazel-eyed dream would pull his pants up, never saying a word to indicate the scene was over, and he'd leave the club looking just as angry as he walked in.

Once, Damon sipped his whiskey, smirking over the rim as his latest obsession turned around, giving the man of his choosing an ear full, screaming that his hand was limper than the girl that tried to give him his first handjob. Damon took note. Perhaps his latest desire swung both ways. Regardless, Damon has watched long enough to understand that one, this boy likes to act out and has no issues having a tantrum when things don't go his way. Two, his ass is the roundest, plumpest gem that he has ever laid eyes on, and Damon has seen more asses than a public toilet, though not necessarily touched or played with them all. And third, whatever this boy comes into the club seeking, Damon believes he hasn't yet been shown what his body desires, and Damon is ready to fulfil that need.

***

Micah steps into the club, wondering whether, at this point, it's worth his time. Since leaving home, he's finally been able to step out and live his life without fear of being shipped off to military school or a conversion camp. His parents threatened him with either whenever he showed signs of being gay. He always knew in his heart they'd follow through with it. Once he settled into his apartment, his parents a speck of dust in his rearview mirror and officially out of his life, Micah put on the only decent shirt and jeans he owned and went to the highest-ranked BDSM club in town.

At the age of twenty-five, he knew what he liked, even if he hadn't been able to partake in it. He was gay, through and through. Sex with women was a way to prove to his parents that he had changed his ways, seen the light and accepted the path that didn't result in his soul burning in hell. He was always drunk enough during the act that he never finished, whiskey dick being his excuse, too gay to keep it up being the truth. Although Micah is new to this scene, he knows two things irrefutably. The first, he loves to take it. The bigger the better. If he is going to bend over, the guy has to be packing enough to have him limping home and feeling it for days to come. The second, what Micah is seeking and has yet to find, is someone who can satisfy his deeper needs. Someone to settle his racing mind. He's done his research. He doesn't want some burly guy to whip his back like a slave being punished, or someone who will slap him around to get him in line. Pain and punishment aren't what he's interested in. He wants 'good' pain, a satisfying reward.

He looks around the room, seeing a few familiar faces. Men who, to some degree, helped him achieve what he was looking for. Others were as disappointing as the time he first had sex with a girl, wondering what the hype was all about. He's never had sex with anyone from the club. Never found anyone who looks as though they can handle him, which perhaps may be why, at times, he's more on edge during his visits. He's got pent-up energy *and* an ass that hasn't been pounded in over a month. On this particular night, he instantly notices that the brunet who catches his eye every time he walks in is nowhere to be seen.

Disappointment isn't the word he wants to use considering he's never spoken to the guy or seen him do anything more than watch what's happening in the club. At this point, Micah's convinced he's either into voyeurism or owns the club and simply likes to enjoy his investment. But during each of his visits, Micah always feels this pull. And when he's followed that tingling Spidey sense, it's led him back to the older—yet not old enough to cause Micah to cringe at the thought of grey pubes and the need for Viagra to perform—brunet.

Perhaps he *has* been interested in why this stranger has been eyeing him off yet has been too much of a coward to make a move. And *perhaps* tonight he is a little annoyed that although he always has an audience, he won't have his number one fan watching whatever he decides to do.

He walks further into the room. A twink is being edged on a Saint Andrew's Cross; that could be fun. He ignores the two bears spit-roasting someone in a gimp outfit. Not his scene, taste, or something he'd do in public. There is a guy twice Micah's age being used as a human pincushion. The needles create floral art on his skin. He recoils at the thought of partaking in that sort of pain and decides to head over to the bar. With the club's drink limit, he knows anything he orders will be for the taste or a light buzz. The club implements a safety-first policy, prohibiting anyone from ordering enough to become intoxicated.

With a whiskey in hand, he spins, leaning his back against the bar, and his eyes land on the sight before him. Micah only just avoids spitting out his drink. He spots the brunet, the one he's been fascinated with for weeks, sitting in some sort of loveseat. The guy looks huge compared to the last time he saw him. Muscles bulging from the tight black T-shirt, though not the kind of bulge that would result from a gym obsession. His jeans look even tighter.

Or, perhaps what makes this mysterious man look like the type who could manhandle him as if he weighed nothing at all, is the small, fragile-looking creature curled into himself on his lap.

The kid looks younger than Micah, though that could be because of the onesie he's wearing. Rule number one of the club: don't judge other people's kinks. But this one has Micah's eyes rolling. He takes another sip of his drink and pretends to be searching the room for his choice of prey for the evening, but his eyes are back on the brunet in an instant, and he's surprised when their eyes lock.

The brunet smirks at him, fucking smirks as though he can read Micah's thoughts, which at the moment, he can't make sense of. The brunet runs his fingers through the younger guy's hair, whispering into his ear, all without breaking eye contact with Micah. Suddenly, the baby-looking kid nods his head and uncurls himself before walking into the centre of the room. Micah follows long enough to see if the kid has someone with him or not, and that's when he notices the bright red handprints on the kid's ass where the onesie has risen between his cheeks.

He's seen enough.

Turning back around so he's now facing the bar, Micah downs his drink and orders another.

★★★

Damon stays seated. He studies the body language of the raven-haired man. Damon hoped he would come tonight, to bear witness to what Damon has to offer, and from the way those hazel eyes were zoning in on him, he knows his plan worked.

Dmitri is an old play-partner of his, though they've never fucked. Their roles have always been simply Daddy and Little. A cuddle here. A spanking there. A firm, yet nurturing voice telling Dmitri how good he is and offering him special rewards like reading time or playing with toys. That doesn't mean Damon hasn't had sex with a Little in the past if that's their kink. Who is he to shame them when it's his purpose to bring their desires to life?

But this guy. This brooding, headstrong man looks as though he has the softest ass the gay gods have ever created, and Damon already knows he's more than a place to stick his dick. He waits a few more minutes before he stands, holding himself firm as he makes his way over to the bar.

"Same for you, sir?" the bartender asks him. Damon smiles, pleased that all the staff know his order.

"Thanks, Harry. And another of whatever he's having." Damon nods to the man standing beside him who hasn't dared to look up from his glass.

"Not interested. But I'll take the drink," the guy mumbles at him.

This is one of the reasons why Damon loves this club; the music is loud enough to talk privately, but not deafening to the point where he has to yell directly into the ear of the person he's talking to.

"Don't even know what I'm offering." Damon smirks into his drink as he takes a sip of his top-shelf whiskey with three ice cubes.

"If it's anything like what I just saw, not my thing."

"Ah, so you were watching me." Damon leans on his elbow that's resting on the bar, eyes boring into the slightly shorter man.

Mmm, he likes that.

"Not watching. Was scouting the room for what I'm after."

He nods his head a few times. "Maybe you don't know *what* you're after."

This seems to catch the man's attention. The bar is well-lit compared to the rest of the club; it offers Damon a chance to study the soft freckles that litter the man's face. They would almost be missed if one wasn't looking hard enough. He's brought out of his daydreaming thoughts as the man he's fascinated with turns to face him directly, eyebrows raised, tongue swiping across his lip before he bites it.

"I do know that what I want, you can't offer. You *think* you know me, but I ain't like the others that walk through that door."

"I know you want to be spanked. I know that you come in here searching for a release that doesn't involve an orgasm and, more times than not, you walk out even more on edge than you were when you came in here." Damon knows he's pushing it at this point, but he can sense that's what this man wants, to be pushed. He leans in, his mouth grazing the man's ear, pleased to see he doesn't recoil. "I can give you that and so much more. Because I know that deep down, all you need is *Daddy* to tell you what *a good boy* you're being for him."

★★★

Micah's mouth goes dry as the whispered words invade his ear. He has been trying to play hard to get through the whole exchange, especially once he realised this smug Himeros god has an ego larger than his own. Of course, Micah is interested, but what he saw tonight, that sure as shit isn't what he has in mind.

The words 'good boy' and 'Daddy', though never said to him endearingly or sexually, reignites a flame inside of him, one that has been slowly dying. The words act like gasoline being thrown onto an open fire. He tries to swallow. Tries to pretend he doesn't have a half-chub after the smell of whiskey floats off the warm, whispering breath against his ear. From a voice that lowered to a soft velvet tone that made him want to drop his pants then and there.

No. Micah isn't the kind to do as he's told. He's the one who seeks out what he wants.

He takes a step back. His eyes cast to the floor, licking his lips before he finally looks up, and locks in with the greenest eyes he has ever seen.

"I get it. You're hotter than a ten and probably never get told no. But I can promise you, what I want, you can't give me."

Why is he doing this?

Why can't he talk to the guy the same way he does with all the other meatheads at this club and tell him exactly what he's looking for?

He looks the guy up and down one last time before walking off towards the spanking benches, where he finds Patrick, who he knows can give him somewhat of a decent flogging.

He marches over, gives Patrick the nod and then drops his pants. They've done this before; he doesn't have to tell him how hard he wants it or what his safe words are. Traffic lights, plain and simple. His dick presses flush against the leather as he kneels on the cushioned leg rests. His elbows lean in place, the bench essentially putting him in the doggy position with a place to rest his head.

The paddle starts landing its blows. One by one. Five seconds apart. Micah feels the sting of soft leather. Patrick knows how to land a spanking. He knows to stay in one spot for a few hits before moving on to the next. But Micah's mind won't settle. The quietness that he searches for is nowhere to be found, but what he does feel on top of the warm heat of his ass is the feeling of being watched.

Micah turns his head to the right and there he is, the one who claims to be able to give him everything he wants. He is sitting back in the large loveseat, sipping his whiskey, eyes focused only on him. It's not his ass that the brunet is looking at, no, those sparkling green eyes are zoned in on his face.

Without considering the ramifications, Micah says, "Red," and Patrick stops. He knows Patrick is waiting for an explanation, a reason for the abrupt end to their scene but he couldn't give two shits about the bald, bearded wannabe Dom.

Instead, Micah stands, his pants still around his ankles, not caring that his flaccid dick is on display for the whole club to see. He shuffles towards the loveseat, his eyes never breaking contact with the man who is, without question, the most experienced person in this room. Without asking, he lays his body over the brunet's lap, so his ass is facing up, begging to be turned as red as the man's lips.

"I like it hard. I like it so that I don't have to think or remember. I want to be able to finally relax." Micah keeps his eyes on the couch in front of him, where his elbows are resting on the cushion.

He comes to this club because he no longer has to hide who he is from those around him. He no longer has to suppress his desires. Perhaps that's why when he was lying on the cold, black leather—his body screaming to be touched by the man he daydreams about every time he knows he is going to visit this club—he realised that he was once again denying his body what it wants.

A warm hand that feels as soft as silk begins to rub soothing circles against his right cheek, then his left, as though to alleviate the existing marks.

"What's your safe word?" the sultry voice asks.

For some reason, he suddenly feels too shy to look the brunet in the eye.

"Traffic lights. Red, stop. Yellow, ease up. Green, good to go," he recites, if only to reassure the man he's lying on top of that he understands how they work.

"Hmm, *good boy.*"

There it is again. The words instantly have him trembling. If the other man could see his face, Micah knows his cheeks would be matching the shade of his ass.

"Here is what's going to happen. I'm going to spank this beautifully rounded ass until the song changes."

Micah gulps. This club tends to play songs that can last for five minutes, using remixes to help with the vibe of the room.

"At the end, if you're happy with my work, *I'm* going to get a reward."

Micah's breath shutters as he asks, "Wh-what kind of reward?"

Once again, that warm whiskey breath whispers against his ear, "Your name."

As the brunet sits back up, pulling away from his ear, the man's beautiful, seductive voice echoes in his head. Micah is lost in it when he feels the first smack on his left cheek.

His breath hitches.

Smack.

His back arches.

Smack.

The bare skin on skin feels so sexy.

Smack.

His ass begins to tingle.

Smack.

His skin is heating.

Smack.

The breeze from the AC causes goosebumps to prickle his exposed skin.

Smack.

His body trembles.

Smack.

His stomach fills with butterflies, sending shockwaves throughout his entire body.

Smack.

The music playing in the club quietens.

Smack.

The sound of the man's hand hitting his ass is blissful.

Smack.

Finally…Micah feels at peace.

LITTLE ONE

★★★

When the song changes, Damon stops.

His breathing is laboured. He knows he's in control, but he takes a moment to slowly breathe in…hold it…and breathe out. His body buzzes with energy that he hasn't felt in a very long time. The sight before him is glorious. This raven-haired man's porcelain skin is now a blushing shade of cherry red. Somehow, after the spanking it endured, the voluptuous cheeks are even more plump and rounded.

He wants to kiss them, gently on each cheek, and feel their burning heat against his lips. Instead, he runs his fingers through slicked-back hair, not caring about the gel that's matting his fingers. Damon swears he hears a purr as the man's body vibrates from his hair being played with. His fingers continue to massage, hoping the sound continues.

"You're such a good boy. So proud of the way you took your spanking." He prides himself on being a Daddy. It's the label he gave himself and tells his partners to call him. Although when he said it earlier in the evening, it didn't spark the response he was hoping for from the agitated man. He decides to test the waters while his *hopefully* new play partner is sated and boneless in his lap.

"Daddy loves all the marks he has left on your beautiful behind. I'm going to rub some cream on it to help soothe the heat." It's only as he leans a little to the side to reach for the table beside his love seat, the one that holds essentials such as lube, aloe vera,

Sorbolene, condoms, and a few toys, does Damon notice the hard cock rubbing into his thigh. He ignores it, though it's a feat.

Based on their brief conversation, Damon decides to go with the Sorbolene. It's obvious Micah loves the afterburn just as much as the spanking itself. This thought alone is why he opts out of the aloe vera.

As Damon carefully rubs the moisturiser into each cheek, a moan falls from the man's lips, which are pink and swollen from being bitten.

"Micah."

The word is spoken so randomly and out of nowhere that Damon almost misses it.

"What was that?" he asks kindly.

"'M name…'s Micah."

A smile brighter than a kid who wakes Christmas morning spreads across his face. He did it. He gave Micah what he wanted, and he got his reward.

"Thank you, Micah. I'm Damon."

***

Micah allows the name to fall from his lips, though he does it silently so as not to break the spell that has been cast between himself and…*Damon*.

For the first time, Micah isn't sure where to go from here. He's never found himself hard after being spanked.

Could it be because it was bare-handed spanking rather than the instruments other men have used on him in the past?

Could it be from the words of endearment that followed? He always preferred silence during play with others.

Or perhaps, it's because of Damon himself? This mysterious man Micah constantly wonders about playing with, curious about his methods and techniques.

He can't deny that Damon ticks all the right boxes for him.

Handsome, in a way that Micah never thought he'd find in an older man. Green eyes. A toned body that indicates self-care, not self-obsessed, and a kind, yet flirtatious smile. Slightly cocky, and he knows it, too. Confident, and Micah is betting that comes with a side of possessiveness. Tall, and he can't understand why that suddenly has his engine revving. Muscular, but not in a juicehead kind of way, just enough that Micah hopes Damon will have the ability to hold him against a wall if the situation presents itself.

But besides all that, everything that happened was so different to his experiences in the past. For the first time, Micah gave up his control. He voiced what he wanted and then let the rest play out how Damon saw fit.

And it worked. He was finally able to relax. To shut down.

It felt freeing.

His dick seemed to have agreed, which has thankfully calmed down, understanding that unfortunately, playtime is over.

Micah pushes himself off Damon's lap in a way that shields his dick from everyone around him, which is pointless considering the free show he gave only moments before.

He coughs. "Um, thanks."

As Micah zips up and buttons his jeans, he flicks his eyes towards Damon and catches the coy smile on the brunet's face.

"Would it be too forward of me to give you my number?" Damon asks him.

He shrugs, unable to trust his voice to give the right answer. He hands his phone over and it's only seconds later that it is being passed back to him. Micah looks at the contact and number in his phone, seeing that it's real.

"Thought you would have put your name as Daddy," he says as a joke, but Damon doesn't laugh.

"I'll leave that up to you. But perhaps you need to understand the significance of that title before you throw it around."

Damon stands, long fingers reaching out and touching Micah's chin, guiding it up so their eyes lock.

"Thank you for letting me show you a glimpse of what I can offer you, Micah. I do hope to hear from you." The swipe of Damon's thumb against his chin is the last thing Micah feels before the brunet walks past him and towards the exit.

He exhales, unaware he is holding his breath. A small part of him feels like Damon forgot something before he left. A handshake. Perhaps a hug. Or is it something more that Micah's body is seeking? Something he's never offered anyone before.

He looks down at his phone, the lock screen telling him it's time to go if he wants to be able to function for work tomorrow.

Holy shit. What a night.

Chapter 2

A Conversation

Micah waits three days. He doesn't want to seem desperate, because he isn't, but he also doesn't know how often Damon frequents the club. He tries not to think about Damon using his skills or other valuable parts of his body on any guy who walks up to him and asks. The thought alone starts to make his blood boil, a sensation he isn't used to when dealing with play partners.

During those three days, every time he went to sit, the tenderness of his ass cheeks instantly reminded him of the event that brought on the discomfort, which he loved just as much as he did the spanking.

He finishes up at work at the small bookstore that was hiring when he first moved to town. He had no experience, but the lovely old lady behind the counter was willing to give him a chance. His sole responsibility was to organise books on the shelves and return the books people dumped in the wrong spot when they decided not to buy them.

It was easy, routine, and gave him a chance to broaden his imagination a little as he began to spend his lunch breaks reading one of the many books the store had to offer.

Now, he's more hands-on, talking to customers and handling purchases. Honestly, besides his name not being on the title, it feels as though he owns the place.

Once home, he takes a seat on the couch, his denim jeans brushing against his tender skin, causing a hiss to escape as he unlocks his phone. Micah opens a new text message.

"Screw it," he says as he writes exactly what's on his mind.

Micha

> Alright, why is the term Daddy so important to you? I mean, after seeing that twink on your lap, it only sets off some red flags if you ask me. You got a thing for kids?

Only a few seconds later, as he goes to turn his screen off, he receives a reply.

Damon

> Hello, Micah. How are you? I'm good, thank you for asking. How is your behind feeling today?

He rolls his eyes.

> Sore and yellow. I was after a shade that works better with my skin tone.

> Also, how'd you know it was me?

> Perhaps we can work on better colouring next time. Besides, a more detailed discussion will need to happen if we do continue to play together.

> Honestly, it could only have been you. Anyone else who has my number understands my title.

> Yeah, I ain't playing with anyone that wants me to be their child.

The next message surprises him.

> Micah, if you are unable to understand why people choose to partake in particular kinks, understand why they like it or need it, then perhaps I'm not the person you should be playing with. Kinks are never to be shamed, and from your attitude, it sounds to me that you simply can't grasp why a person would choose to be a Little, or even in my case, thrive on being a Daddy.

Micah reads the message three times to try and understand it, only to panic and accidentally-on-purpose hit the call button once he realises what Damon is insinuating.

The dial tone begins to ring and Micah realises what he's doing. "Shit. Shit. Fuck." He goes to hang up, however, the line connects, and he instantly calms from the simple way Damon greets him hello.

"Sorry. I didn't mean to…call or, whatever." Except he did, he just has no idea how to handle himself now that Damon can hear the frantic confusion in his voice.

There is a faint chuckle on the other end of the line that surprisingly doesn't frustrate Micah. It makes him want more.

"Look. This is…it's new to me," he outright admits. "I've seen the videos, I know what I want, but getting it…that's only something I've just begun doing, okay?"

"By videos, I assume you're referring to pornographic videos?"

"Yeah…what else would I be talking about?"

"Perhaps educational ones. Talks on BDSM. Videos on training to be a Submissive."

"Submis—no way. I'm not bowing down to anyone."

There is a sigh of exhaustion on the other end.

"You really are new to this world." It's said with a tone of understanding more than accusation.

Micah goes to bite back, but Damon continues to speak.

"I'm thirty-five years old, Micah," Damon states, sounding tired rather than frustrated.

He tries to quickly do the math. Ten-year age gap. That's not too bad, right? Though to be honest, he's never ventured more than three or four years older.

"I knew when I stepped into the BDSM world that I wanted to be a Daddy or Daddy Dom if you will, because I like to take on a parental role. A nurturing role. It doesn't mean that I want to fuck a child, Micah. It doesn't mean that I like to be with younger men. It's simply a masculine term for someone who likes to offer guidance and support in their partner's personal development."

Micah lets the words marinate. He dissects them and tries to understand them.

"It means, Micah, that when I play, I want to put your needs before my own. I want to give you what you need physically, mentally, and sexually, and afterwards, I'm going to insist on aftercare. That is one rule I will not break and something I have noticed that you do not partake in."

"The hell's aftercare?" He never saw that in any of the videos he watched.

"The cream I put on your hot little cheeks, that's aftercare. Checking in to make sure you were okay, or that you were safe to leave. Scenes can leave a person feeling vulnerable, emotional, and sometimes over-energised or drained. It's my duty to make sure it's safe for you to drive, to be alone, and that your mental state is not going to cause a drop that can leave you in a state of panic. *That's* aftercare."

Micah thinks back to the first time he visited the club. He left as soon as the flogging was over, feeling like he had enough energy to rob a bank. However, the second he got behind the wheel of his car, he began to shake. His heart rate escalated, and his breathing was erratic. Micah put it down to finally being able to try something he had been craving for years, but perhaps that wasn't the case.

"So, what you're saying is, if I want you to spank me again, I have to call you Daddy and let you ask me a bunch of questions before I go home?" His sarcasm is in full force.

Damon ignores it. "Do you want me to spank you again, Micah?"

He swallows. "...yes"

"Do you want anything else from me, Micah?"

He can't ignore the twitch in his jeans.

"That depends. Are you a top or a bottom?"

"I think we both know the answer to that," Damon says, and Micah pictures that cocky smirk of his.

"Look. This seems a bit much. More than anything I've tried before."

"Can I tell you something, Micah?"

"Don't see why not. You're telling me everything else."

"I've been watching you, seeing what you come to the club for, what you enjoy and what makes you get up and leave. I've seen that type of behaviour before, that energy that makes you feel like your skin is itching but when you go to scratch it, it's deeper, beneath the surface."

There is a pause, and he wonders if that's the end of Damon's story.

"You have that itch, Micah." *Okay, guess he has more to share.* "And I think it goes deeper than needing a spanking or two."

"Well, yeah. Wouldn't mind being fucked so hard that I need an ice bath when I'm done."

"How did it feel when you saw Dmitri on my lap?"

"Am I meant to know who the hell Dmitri is?" He's only played with Damon once, but for some strange reason, he doesn't want to be thinking of anyone else being on that warm, safe, comfortable lap.

"The Little," Damon tells him. "Dmitri came to me, wanting a Daddy to help him keep his Little in line. He wanted spankings when he misbehaved and praise and cuddles when he was a good boy."

He scoffs. "And who decided if he misbehaved or not?"

"Mostly me. But at times, Dmitri too. His job takes a toll on him and his Little allows him to wind down, decompress. Though at times, if he doesn't go into that head space frequently enough, he does something to hurt himself, to self-destruct. Either by drinking too much, overspending money he doesn't have or sleeping with someone he shouldn't. That's when he needed a punishment."

"Why are you telling me this? And should you be telling me this? I feel like you're breaking some doctor-patient confidentiality thing."

"I'm telling you because I *wanted* you to see me with Dmitri. I asked him to come out that night even though I hadn't done a scene with him for close to three years. Thankfully, he was available."

"Why the hell did you do that? Wanted to make me jealous or something?"

"No, Micah. I wanted to show you because I think you too have a Little that needs to come out and play."

With that, Micah hangs up the phone.

Micah storms into the club on a mission. It's a Friday. He never goes on a Friday because the place is crowded, and the excess of bodies makes him uncomfortable. And sure, he could have gone to another club, but perhaps a part of him hopes Damon will be sitting in his corner so that he can witness what Micah has set out to do.

It's two nights after their phone call and in no way is he going to let Damon have the upper hand.

No way is he into being a Little.

He doesn't need someone telling him what he can and can't do. He left a life of that behind him, with his parents dictating how he had to live his life, how to act and who to date.

It's hard to pinpoint the right person for the job through the body of people, but he knows what he's looking for.

Tall. Rough. Muscular. Powerful.

And then he sees the person who ticks all those boxes. Someone he's never seen before, which is perfect.

Micah walks up to a shirtless guy. A chest harness is strapped around his pecs that has braces that clip onto his black jeans, and leg harnesses around each thigh. He's blond, with eyes a colour that Micah can't identify in the low lighting, and a cheeky smirk.

"Ey, wanna play?" he outright asks.

"Depends, what you got in mind?"

"Thought you could flog my ass raw and then I could fuck yours." He has no idea if the guy is a bottom, most men who claim to be Dominant aren't, but these days it seems every guy he meets is verse.

"I could be down for that." The guy stands and Micah has to tilt his head back to keep his eyes level with the guy. "Name's Dante."

"Don't care. Let's go."

He walks straight towards a private room. It's clear Damon isn't here, which means there is no need to let these voyeurs get off while he does. To his surprise, there is a room free. He walks in. Daniel, or whatever the guy's name is, closes the door behind them and the room goes instantly quiet.

Soundproof, that's handy.

"Pretty simple. Follow the traffic light system. Make sure to leave a mark," Micah explains as he unbuckles his jeans. He turns around so his ass is the only thing the guy gets to see.

There is a couch and a St. Andrew's Cross in the room. Along the wall are a variety of toys, and below it is a tray with cleaning wipes, disinfectant, lube and condoms. Micah places his hands on the wooden cross, legs spread, and waits for what he wants.

"Ass already looks a little tender. Ya sure you want me to add to it?"

"Would I have asked you to if I didn't? Come on, hurry up," he orders.

The first hit takes him by surprise. The wooden paddle not only burns against his bruised skin, but the vibration sends a shock wave up his spine and down his legs.

Before he can adjust, another blow comes. It hurts, just like he wanted.

No one tells him how to live his life.

Wack.

No one tells him when he needs punishment.

Wack.

He isn't someone who needs babying.

Wack.

He doesn't need someone to be soft with him.

Wack.

He needs it to hurt.

Wack.

He needs it to take away the past.

Wack.

Take away the pain.

Wack.

To make him forget.

Wack.

"RED."

Micah can barely hold himself up, the throb and ache in his ass causes his legs to tremble.

"Hey man, you good?"

All he does is nod his answer, not ready to speak.

"He would do something to hurt himself, to self-destruct…" Damon's words ring in his head.

"You-you're still going to fuck me, right?"

"Afterwards, I'm going to insist on aftercare." Micah could swear Damon was in the room, his voice is so clear.

It dawns on him that this guy isn't offering to give him any care, any cream, he's just pushing for his own pleasure.

"Yeah…yeah, 'm ready." He finally catches his breath. He pulls himself away from the cross, and notices his playmate already leaning over the couch, ass on display.

All Micah can do is look at the tanned ass with hair that trails up from his thighs and vanishes just above the base of his cheeks. He isn't even hard.

He spits on his hand.

He's harsh with his strokes but he's used to it. His dick needs to hurry up and get with the program.

"I want to put your needs before my own."

Suddenly the rough blond before him is a tall brunet who's looking over his shoulder, piercing green eyes watching him in wonderment.

"Is this really what you want, Micah? What you need?"

"Might not be what I want, but it'll feel good."

"Hold up, what do you mean you don't want this?" Dante questions.

Shit.

Damon's all in his head, has him saying shit out loud.

"It's fine, whatever. Let's do this." The only thing is, his dick has other plans. He's been rubbing it for a good five minutes and it's still as soft as when he tried to watch straight porn.

"Look man, I get it." The guy pulls his jeans back up, not even giving Micah a chance to protest before he continues speaking. "You might have thought it was hot when you were drunk and made out with your best friend, but if you can't get it up, it's safe to say you're as straight as an arrow."

"What the—" The door to the private room opens and his failed conquest walks out.

"I'm so gay my father tried to brainwash me to be straight," he yells out, though the words get lost in the soundproof room.

Showered, he stands looking at himself in the full-length mirror, his head twisting around to see the bruises left on his ass.

It's ugly.

Deep, maroon blemishes, some purple. Broken skin in areas where blood has dripped and dried. Based on the way each hit had been random, not at all thought about or calculated, Micah concludes that the guy had no idea how to spank or had any experience in the matter. The worst part is, he knows how bruising works, and this is only going to get worse over the next few days.

At least the bruises from Damon were pretty, to say the least. They had begun to fade by the fourth night, but they still gave a story, one better than what his ass is saying now.

He eases himself onto his mattress, wearing nothing but soft cotton boxers and pulls up his laptop. He can't even blame what he's about to do on alcohol since not a single drop has entered his bloodstream. As he goes to the search engine, he types in 'Little BDSM'.

He scrolls and clicks. He reads and cringes, and then he takes in the information that seems relevant.

A Little is a person who identifies with or enjoys exhibiting a child-like mindset and/or behaviour. Their relationships may or may not include a power exchange component. A Little may also incorporate ageplay, where they participate in acting a different age from their physical age. Such play is not necessarily sexual in nature and can often be cathartic for the parties involved.

A Little may also go by the term babyboy/girl, which identifies a person who seeks a parental and/or nurturing figure in relationships.

These roles have not only been used for play, sexual or otherwise, but can also be used for therapeutic tendencies.

LITTLE ONE

A child is vulnerable, their mind is susceptible to learning and can therefore help with difficult situations an adult may have trouble processing, understanding or remembering from the past. This is where a Little can help their Big when having trouble moving forward.

He reads the information a few more times before he picks up his phone and shoots off a text message, not even caring that it's almost one in the morning.

Micah

> You said being a Little would help me. Why?

Watching his screen, he's disappointed to see that the three dancing dots don't appear. He exhales. Damon's probably asleep, or he could be with someone. Playing with them. Having sex with them. Sleeping beside them.

The thought makes his stomach nauseous, the threat of bile rising within.

His phone buzzes in his hand, the lock screen showing a reply twenty minutes after he sent the message. Maybe Damon isn't with someone then, he hopes. He opens the message and understands that the reason it took so long for Damon to reply is that he wrote an essay.

Damon

> You walk into the club looking as though you hate everyone in the room. You look for the toughest person, thinking that what you're after is pain. But when you stand up and leave, you're still angry, frustrated, because that anger is directed at someone you can't get angry at. An ex perhaps. Yourself. I don't know, and maybe you don't either, but the pain is your punishment, the release is your gift and that is something you're not allowing yourself to enjoy.

Damon's message hits him where it hurts because this stranger has him figured out.

This time, he sees the three dots. He waits. Damon didn't exactly give him an answer but even still, he isn't sure he can come up with some form of a reply either.

Damon

> I can give you that release, Micah. I can spank that gorgeous bottom until it's as pink as your hole and I could fuck you so hard you have a limp. But neither of those will be enough because you'll still be angry and you'll still push for each spanking to be a little harder and each fuck to be a little rougher until eventually, you get hurt.

This time he hits the call button on purpose. He wants to hear Damon's voice. Within two rings, the line connects.

"Hello, Micah." Damon's voice is sleepy, husky, but Micah gets the sense he was wide awake when he sent the message.

He swallows. "How do you know all this? You don't know anything about me and yet you're writing to me like you've known me for years and have all the answers."

"Because, Micah, that's what being a Daddy is about. I analyse people. I learn to read their cues so that I can give them what they want and what they need before they, themselves, even know what to ask for."

Micah clicks on an image as he scrolls on his computer, the phone still to his ear. It portrays a guy around his age, dressed in comfortable pyjamas with Disney Superheros on them, smiling as he sits on some other guy's lap, looking not that much older while being read to.

"Can I propose something, Micah?" The question breaks through the silence.

"Can probably guess what it's going to be, but sure."

"Every weekend, unless of course, you work, but if not, every Friday you come to my house, we eat together, talk, get to know each other. On Saturday, I'll fuck you and spank you from sunup to sundown, if that's what you wish, but on Sundays…Daddy wants to spend time with his Little One on Sundays."

He gulps.

"Do you think you could try this? Is this something you want?"
Is it?

Is this some lost childhood he is searching for? Some father figure to replace the one he never had? Is it a way to feel loved even though Micah believed he never would, the words of his parents embedded into his mind?

Damon is making it sound so easy, so simple. He's speaking as though Micah giving himself over to someone he's just met and trusting them, being vulnerable and open around them, a feeling he has avoided for years to protect himself, would be beneficial.

"And if I say yes?"

"Then we draw up a contract and we start next weekend."

"A contract?"

"Yes, Micah. A way for me to know what you want from me and what I want from you. The rules, the punishments, your limits."

Suddenly the sex doesn't sound all that sexy.

"The contract is our promise to each other and ourselves."

"And if I want out?"

"Say the word and we stop. Contract gets ripped up and we part ways."

He adjusts himself on the mattress and hisses in discomfort.

"Are you okay?"

"Yeah, just my ass, it's…whatever."

"You are in pain? The tenderness should have eased by now."

"Was, ah, was someone else."

There is silence. It drags on long enough that Micah checks to see if the line has disconnected.

"Is that why you messaged me? Did something happen that made you consider trying this role?" He isn't sure what to say, but Damon must take his silence as the answer. "I'm free tomorrow. If you'd like, we can meet. Talk. The ball is in your court, Micah. You're in control."

"Only until I sign it over to you."

"No, Micah. That's where you're wrong. You will always be in control. You will always be the one to decide when things start and stop, whether it be based on your behaviour or your desires, that is up to you."

Jesus. Micah thought he knew everything there was about this world. Understood what it involved, how to handle it, and how to take pleasure from it. Now, listening to Damon speak, his experience and confidence obvious, it's clear he hasn't even crossed the starting line.

"I'll do it."

"Do what? You need to learn to use your words, Micah."

"I'll meet with you. Sign a contract. I'll be your Little."

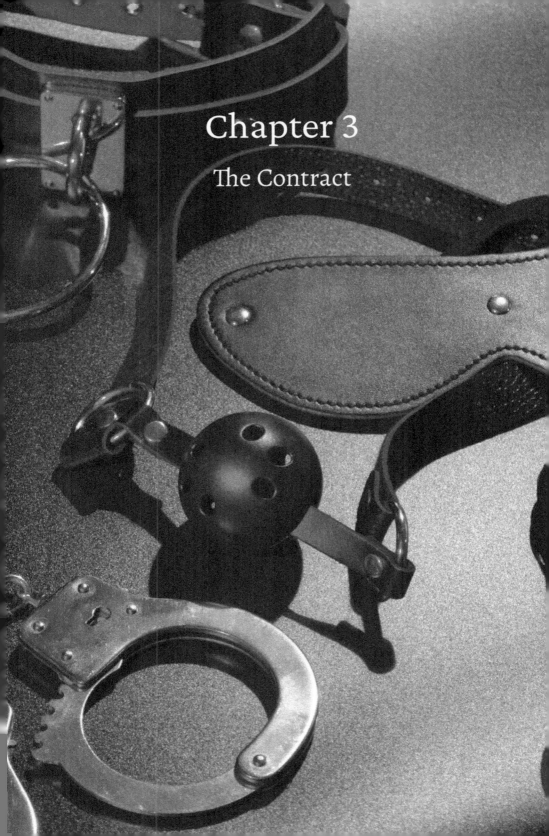

Chapter 3
The Contract

RACHEL O'ROURKE

For some reason, Damon feels nervous, which is strange because he hasn't felt anything like this in almost a decade. His mind and body are always synced, always aware of what's about to happen. But with Micah, it could go either way.

He sits at a table in the corner of a café's outdoor garden not too far from the club he and Micah frequent. Being that he isn't sure where Micah lives, he figures the location isn't too far for Micah to travel to since it's an area he regularly visits.

Perhaps his nerves stem from the fact that Micah is new. Green. A true partner that will test Damon's abilities in teaching and giving. Or, it could have to do with the fact that one look at Micah drives him wild.

Shaking the thought, he takes a sip of his Americano, eying the paperwork sitting in an envelope in front of him. He looks up and is pleased to see that Micah has arrived, the younger man looking around the café in search of him.

Damon raises his hand and Micah opens the doors that lead to the courtyard. He has studied the way Micah's right knee juts out as he walks, giving him not so much a limp, but a swagger with each step. Damon could watch this man walk all day; it is not only captivating but sexy as hell. He wonders if it's a medical condition or from taking a pounding so hard it's affected his walk. Sayings essentially have to arise from somewhere, generally created from facts and experiences. *Fuck me so hard I can't walk*; it has surely happened before.

"Micah. Thank you for coming. Please, sit." He gestures to the chair in front of him. His right leg is crossed over his left, and he's dressed in his loose-fitted button-up and black slim-fit khaki pants.

"Would you like a drink?" He signals for the waitress before Micah answers.

"Ah, coffee. Black. Four sugars," Micah tells the waitress once she arrives.

"And two apple cinnamon muffins, please," Damon adds.

Once alone, Damon removes his sunglasses, the clouds now covering the sun and the trees casting them in the shade.

"Find the place okay?"

"Not that hard to use maps on my phone."

A wiseass. Damon likes it.

"Okay. I suppose small talk isn't your thing." He pushes the envelope toward Micah who goes to take it, stopping when two muffins are placed on the small stone-top table.

"Thank you, Shannon," Damon offers before looking back toward Micah. "It's okay. They're discrete here."

Micah takes the envelope and removes the ten-page document. "What, you bring all your sexual conquests here?"

He chuckles. "No. But I've visited while a partner has disobeyed or acted out. They understand our world. Understand that Daddies must do things in public that society would judge or frown upon."

"You saying you spanked someone here?"

He nods. "Among other things." He takes another sip of his coffee. Micah's arrives just as he sets his cup back down.

"Read it over. I'm sure you have questions, as do I." And with that, he waits.

He enjoys the cool breeze in his hair, a curl falling loose from his high-top combed-back style. He eats his muffin and studies Micah's facial expressions, wondering which part of the contract makes his eyebrows twitch and rise.

Damon finishes his muffin as Micah finishes the last page.

"Where would you like to begin?" he asks, watching as Micah downs his coffee, the liquid most likely cold enough to swallow in one sitting.

"By me signing this contract, it means we're exclusive?"

"I don't share, Micah. If you sign that, it means you are mine and I am yours. When I'm contracted, I don't play, have sex or even sit down like we are now, with other suitors."

"And if we weren't contracted?"

"Then you can do as you please. As can I. And from time to time, we can play. But, as I've learnt in the past, it can be difficult for my Subs to know I'm not available to them twenty-four-seven. To know I'm with someone else. It can mess with their psyche."

"Why? It's just sex."

He smirks.

Yes, he is right, Micah is very new.

"In theory, yes. What you are signing up for are two different yet connected experiences. On the one hand, there will be the playing and the sex which, you're right, on any other day you could have sex with someone, walk away and find someone else a few nights later. However, this isn't any other day. Let me ask you this, what was your favourite toy growing up?"

"What's that have to do with anything?"

"Humour me."

"Fine. It was a toy aeroplane." Micah smiles at the memory. "I'd fly it around everywhere I went, pretending I was on that aeroplane being taken away from where I was."

Things suddenly become a little clearer to Damon.

He pictures a young Micah zooming up and down the hall of his home, envisioning himself on adventures in big cities with buildings taller than him. Or beaches where the sand was white, and the water was clearer than the sky.

He leans forward. "Okay, so…may I hold your hand?" His own hands lay palm open, waiting for consent. Micah rolls his eyes before placing his right hand in his.

"Imagine this is your aeroplane." He fondles Micah's fingers, loving how short and stubby they are. His hand almost looks like a toddler when placed against his own. Micah's hand is now in the form of an aeroplane, his index and ring finger pushed together while his middle finger sits on top, mimicking the nose of the plane. His thumb and pinkie point up and out to replicate the wings. "It's your pride and joy. You clean it and keep it protected. You put it in a safe place at night and wake up knowing nothing happened to it while you were asleep."

He moves Micah's hand to mimic an aeroplane soaring in the air, and that's when he notices a birthmark just above Micah's wrist, so faint he would have missed it if not for the sun's rays bringing it into focus. It's beautiful, Damon thinks. Much like the man it's attached to.

"Now, imagine if someone took your toy away. They used it, maybe you knew this or maybe you didn't. And they had so much fun with it that they didn't want to give it back. Or maybe they also mistreated it. They threw it in random places and didn't bother to clean it or make sure it sparkled and felt appreciated. How does that make you feel?" He releases Micah's hand, so it isn't in the shape of an aeroplane, though he keeps his hand close enough for their fingers to brush ever so slightly.

"I'd be pissed. Devastated. Probably start a fight with them."

"Exactly. Whether it's me that is the aeroplane or you, if someone were to mistreat you, use you in a way that was too rough, or not how *we* play, I'd personally blame myself. And if the tables were turned, if we were enjoying ourselves, but I was then off with another, having just as much fun, well, in hindsight, you could start to assume that everything we had shared may have been a lie, so to speak. Just words in the heat of the moment, and I would never want you to think that anything I've said isn't a true testament to how I feel or what I think of you." He gives Micah time to think, the analogy hopefully enough for him to understand why he doesn't share. It's taken mistakes over the years for him to realise that this is the best for both parties involved.

"So, you're saying we're exclusive but not a couple."

"No. A contract is much different to a relationship, even one that might have a Dominant and Submission role."

"Well, that I can get on board with."

Damon tilts his head to the side, curious. "And why is that?"

"Because I don't do relationships."

"Oh, so you're polyamorous."

"Poly-what?"

"You're unable to be with only one person. You feel love and connections toward multiple people."

"Um, no. I'm whatever you call someone who doesn't have or want connections. And love? That shit doesn't exist."

He believes he's learning the root of Micah's anger.

"Understandable. Let's move forward, shall we? The fact of the matter is, we are exclusive. This is also for our safety."

"Safety?"

"Yes. STDs. HIV. Unless you'd prefer to use protection. I'm open to either."

Micah's throat bobs as he swallows, and Damon can't help the smirk that lifts his lips.

"Nope. Bareback works for me."

"Good," he agrees. "Then we need to present each other with clean test results. It must be dated from today onwards. And I expect a new test result on the first of each month."

"Just say you don't trust me."

"There are levels of trust, Micah. We may agree to be exclusive, but considering I'm the one explaining why that's important, how do I know you'll follow the rule? At the same time, you should want to know that I am keeping my word. Until we have formed a deep enough bond to know that our trust is genuine, repeated tests will not only keep us safe but also be used as proof to eliminate any doubt. Trusting me to control your body is one thing. Trusting me with the safety of your body, well, I would want to hope you're smarter in that area, regardless of how new you are to this scene."

Damon waits. He can see the gears turning in Micah's head. He takes a sip of water and then continues, "If it makes you feel more reassured, I'm also on PrEP."

The blank expression on Micah's face is why he continues. "Pre-exposure prophylaxis. It's merely a drug to help with the prevention of HIV."

Micah suddenly looks uneasy.

"Micah, how old are you?" He keeps his tone light, curious.

"Twenty-five."

He does the math, he's been with younger, but not by much. It's an acceptable age gap but it still makes him wonder.

"Forgive my forwardness, but I get the sense that you've only recently come out."

Micah's eyes go hard. He sits up straight, his chest puffing out like a gorilla who's about to bang on it.

"I'm not some newly confessed homosexual."

Another clue that Damon stores away for later.

"I didn't mean to assume. It's just that most are aware of the drugs and medications available to us these days."

Micah bites his lip, eyes darting around for what he can only assume is the exit.

"Would you like another drink? I can order you something else to eat if you'd like." Again, Damon flags Shannon down before

Micah can answer, and the all-too-cheery auburn-haired waitress walks towards him within seconds.

"Can I please order the chicken and pumpkin risotto for Micah here. I'll have the Cobb Salad, dressing on the side, with two iced teas."

"Certainly, Mr Stone."

He offers her his warmest smile before turning his attention back toward Micah.

"You did it again." Micah folds his arms.

"Did what?" he asks, curious about the sudden closed-off attitude.

"Ordered for me before I even answered."

He bows his head, smiling, feeling slightly embarrassed.

"I'm sorry. Habit. As I said, it's in my nature to want to provide and care for the person I'm with and that can also involve making sure they eat, stay hydrated and even get enough sleep." He reaches out, playing with his sunglasses that are resting on the table before him. "Scenes can take a lot of energy out of a person; without a balanced diet, it can be a lot on the body. And besides, the last thing I want is for you to eat a five-pound steak before I fuck you up against the wall." Damon smirks at the cute blush that spreads across Micah's face and watches as he squirms in his seat and rubs the back of his neck. He grimaces and that's when Damon recalls his bruised cheeks.

"What are you into, Micah? What is it you want from me?" It's his turn to ask some questions. He waits. It's obvious his new play partner isn't used to being asked what he wants, let alone getting it.

"To be honest, I have no clue," Micah finally offers up.

"I'm sure that's not right. You watch porn. I'm assuming that is already a sign of what you get off on."

Micah shrugs, but after a few moments, he finally speaks. "I don't know. Fetish or whatever it's called. Being manhandled 'n used, with the harnesses and whips, I guess."

"I see." He nods his head, smiles, and makes sure to present himself in a manner that proves he doesn't have to be ashamed of anything they speak about. "So, you want to feel as though you have no control. You're being forced to have sex?" he asks.

"What? I don't want rape roleplay. No. No, I just—"

He can see that Micah is getting uncomfortable.

"This is a safe place, Micah. No judgement. In case you haven't noticed, no one is around. Shannon has made sure all other patrons are seated inside while we talk."

He watches Micah look around the courtyard, no doubt taking in his surroundings for the first time since he sat down. Shannon walks out with their food and drinks, a polite smile on her face as she places everything on the table for them.

"Thank you, Shannon," Damon offers as she walks off.

"Look." Micah exhales. "I've spent my whole life having to hide that I was gay so that my parents didn't send me off to military school or worse, some conversion therapy camp." Micah's words seem like a sigh of relief. "Besides the guys I slept with when my parents went away for the weekend or had an event at our local church, my experience has been a little lacklustre up until a few months ago. I finally had enough money saved to leave. I announced to my parents how much I love cock as they cursed me to hell and screamed that I was never welcome back into their home."

"I'm sorry that's what you had to grow up with. That you not only had no support but also no one to talk to or feel yourself around."

"Can't live in the past. Now, I'm finally free. After the brainwashing of how God will spite me, all that fire and brimstone shit that would make any kid scared, I just—" Micah reaches for his iced tea, takes a sip, and his eyebrows rise in surprise. Damon can't help but chuckle as he watches Micah drink half the contents in one long gulp.

"I'll order another. But please, carry on." He catches Shannon's attention through the glass doors, pointing down to the empty glass and waiting for her nod of acknowledgement.

"The fact that I'm sitting here, even considering this…" Micah continues. "I'm used to quick hook-ups and one-night stands. I'm used to no feelings and never seeing the guy again, but for some reason, I can't get you or your stupid words out of my head."

"Is that why you hurt yourself the night you called?" he asks the question, needing the answer so he can understand Micah's mentality in all of this.

"Pfft. Hurt myself? It's not like I fell over a rock."

"No, but you were frustrated and instead of talking to me, you went out and allowed some inexperienced simpleton to mistreat you."

"How'd you know he was inexperienced?"

"Call it a hunch." From the way Micah is leaning more to the right rather than sitting evenly, along with the phone call that led Micah to consider his proposal and agree to meet today, Damon suspects his hunch is right on the money.

"As I said, our conversation had obviously upset you and from what I've gathered, in the past, when you have felt like this, I'm guessing your go-to was drinking. Fighting even, whether it be physically or verbally."

"Is this a therapy session now?"

"No, but BDSM can be. Kinks can unlock therapeutic healing when handled correctly. I'm not saying that's what I'm offering, but it could be why you're searching for something within this world. Even if you aren't aware of it."

Micah finally takes a bite of his food. It makes Damon proud to see him shove a few large forkfuls into his mouth.

"I don't know the details and I don't want to know," Damon continues while Micah eats, his jaw clenching at the thought of someone else not only touching but mistreating that beautiful hind. "It's also not my place. But playing in a scene with someone inexperienced can be dangerous, especially when you're after a certain level of affliction." He pulls himself further into the table, placing the napkin over his lap.

"I can give you bruises. I can leave a mark that you will feel for days, and I can do those things without causing you harm, Micah. Without breaking your tailbone or causing nerve damage. I can do it safely. And sometimes, when we're stuck in our heads, safety is the last thing we are thinking about."

Damon takes a bite of his salad, giving Micah a chance to sit and ponder over all the information they have shared during this meeting.

He doesn't push. He doesn't prod. He sits and eats his meal and as he collects the last of his salad on his fork, Micah finally speaks.

"I freaked out when you told me I should be a Little." Micah keeps his eyes on the empty plate before him.

Removing his napkin from his lap, Damon wipes his mouth clean before placing it on the table.

"To clarify, I never said you *should* be a Little. I merely suggested that you may have one that wants to come out and play."

The eye roll response makes him smirk.

"Still, was weird," Micah clarifies.

"And now?" he questions. "You've asked me about it, so I'm assuming you've looked into it, perhaps thought about it."

Micah shrugs.

Damon is getting awfully good at reading Micah's body cues.

"I read about it. Read what it can do, why people do it." Micah folds his arms. "I'm not wearing a fucking diaper."

"Nobody fucking asked you to." It's that response that seems to impress Micah, who raises his eyebrows and smirks at Damon's quick retort and a hint of attitude.

"You're right though, I knew nothing about you when I made that comment. It was based purely on what I saw when you attended the club. So, forgive me for being so forward. However, after the glimpse into what you've been through, I'm even more certain that having time as a Little will benefit you mentally and sexually."

He raises his hand before Micah can speak.

"No, I'm not talking about sex while you're a Little. *Jesus*. I'm referring to the fact that as you spend time as a Little, it will help your body open to a more rewarding sexual experience. Your mind will be freer and in tune with your body."

"God, I must be desperate." It's a mumbled whisper but Damon catches it. "Fine. I'll do it. But I'm making some changes."

Damon refrains from fist-pumping the air in excitement.

"Of course. Whatever would make you feel more comfortable," he offers.

"Friday nights, we fuck. If you're offering me the spanking I'm apparently looking for, no way are we doing that before you turn me inside out. And, if you *can* whoop my ass properly then I shouldn't be wanting anything else afterwards, *right?*"

"I can accept this change. What else?"

"I'm not submitting. This isn't some 'you tell me what to do and when' situation, okay? I'm a bottom and sometimes I like to take the lead. But I'm not going to bow down at your feet or anything like that."

"For now, this is fine. However, over time, you may find yourself submitting naturally, and I hope that you will allow yourself to do so rather than fight it because you believe it makes you…for lack of a better word, a pussy."

"What? Two Doms can't screw?" Micah asks.

"Oh, they can, but one will always cave in."

"Yeah, I'm not one to cave."

"I believe it," he states. "But submission is a lot like being a trained dog."

Based on the rise of Micah's eyebrows, it's obvious he isn't happy with Damon's analogy.

"Okay, fine. A trained cat."

"That's not any better."

"Just, hear me out." He swallows the last of his drink. "What we're about to agree to is a partnership of the body and mind. You'll let me do things, as in, permit me to put you in compromising positions that sometimes end in a release. That's the body part, the sex."

He studies Micah's face. No change. He assumes it's safe to continue.

"But then there's also the mind part. You'll slowly let me in and begin to do things that I ask, which will never be commands of power or ranking. You'll do them because you feel good, relaxed and you trust me, even if you don't know it yet because obviously, trust builds over time, like training a skittish beast. A small, cuddly, black-furred one." He winks, emphasising the trained kitten comment. "Sooner or later, your mind searches for the release I can provide mentally just as much as your dick does. And that, dear Micah, is why you will eventually want to submit."

Micah shakes his head as a smile slowly spreads across his face. "You got room in there for anything else besides your ego?"

They both laugh.

"I may not be good at many things in life, but this, being a Daddy and fucking, I'm so good I could get paid for it."

He watches Micah move his wrist in a jerking-off motion. It only makes him smile more, excited to prove himself to Micah as they embark on this journey together.

"You're all talk until you prove it."

Damon smirks before moving on to another subject. "What about limits? Toys? Is there anything you want off the table?"

Micah shrugs. "Only the usual hard limits."

"Which are?" Damon checks, knowing they are different for everyone.

"No urine or faeces. No blood or weapons or slapping me around and calling me names and shit."

Damon nods in understanding. He makes a note that praise kink might be something Micah may enjoy.

"Plugs? Blindfold? Rope or cuffs?" Damon asks. "I've seen how comfortable you are with paddles and floggers."

"Yeah, that's all fine."

"What about a gag? Or a cock cage?"

"Why the fuck would I want a cage on my dick?"

"Maybe one day you can find out. But let's keep it simple, shall we? If I have plans to use anything within a scene or during sex, I'll be sure to discuss it with you first so you know what's to be expected. Sound reasonable?"

Micah shrugs. "I guess. Nothing sexier than planning how you're going to have sex."

Damon ignores the sarcasm. This is all new territory for Micah, so small bursts of information will help him respond better than everything at once.

"Is that all?" he checks.

"Last thing. I'm not acting any younger. I'm not going to pretend I'm five. I'm not going to ask you to change a diaper or give me a bottle. Simple as that."

"You're a Little, but not into ageplay. Check."

"Right." Micah coughs as though he's trying to find the courage to continue. "I'll, ah, I'll get tested this week. Send you the results. We do this at your place. If I'm not into it, we pull the plug, contract or not."

"Deal." Damon reaches over, takes the contract and makes a few amendments to match Micah's terms, making note that this is a trial-based contract and adjusting the plans for Friday and Saturday nights. He then passes it over for Micah to check, watching as his striking hazel eyes scan over the words before picking up the pen and signing his name against the section that says Submissive.

Micah slides the contract back, and Damon signs against the line beside the title Dominant. He catches sight of the name beside his. "Michelangelo. I like that."

"Yeah, my mother was despondent that its origin 'he who resembles God' was affiliated with her closeted gay son. So, I started going by Micah."

"I've come across a lot of names over the years. Personally, I believe we're the only ones with the power to create a meaning for our name, no one else."

Although he is hoping for his comment to be endearing, something flashes across Micah's face. Disgust? Jealousy? He takes note that from this moment, with their names both signed, any mention of past partners shall be banned unless needed for information that could affect their play. From here on out, it's only Damon and Micah.

He stands. Micah follows suit.

"May I hug you?" Damon asks.

"Why?" Micah questions.

"You've just signed your body over to me for every weekend for the foreseeable future. I figured a celebratory hug would seem more appropriate than a blow job." He smirks when he sees the lust in Micah's eyes.

"Fine. Though the blowie woulda been better."

His right arm goes over Micah's shoulder, his left linking up from under his armpit. Their height difference allows Micah to bury his face in the nook of his neck, between his shoulder and collarbone.

It's nice. Intimate in its own kind of way.

He takes a deep inhale of Micah's scent. It's a deep, musky smell that reminds him of a burning fire in a wood cabin during the middle of winter, as the snow falls outside while he sips a glass of whiskey. It's a struggle to pull away. His body instantly relaxes in the arms of the slightly smaller man, but he does pull back. They politely say goodbye, planning to meet up again by the following weekend.

The second Micah is out of sight, Damon begins to count down the hours until he can see him again.

Chapter 4

Trial Run; The Sex

RACHEL O'ROURKE

Micah stands in the elevator as it takes him up to the penthouse in one of the most lavish apartment buildings in the heart of the city. The doorman had to scan his keycard for Micah to get access to the level, which took him by surprise.

He has no idea what to expect. All he knows is he's going to be fed and hopefully get railed to the point that he'll forget the dry spell he is in. Ironic considering all the spankings he's taken. The doors open and he steps into what he assumes is Damon's living area.

"No. No membership, no private room. They want to get their dick out, they can pay for it or go home," Damon snaps, angry and assertive, a side Micah hasn't seen before. "Don't call me again. I'm done for the evening." He hangs up.

"Sorry," Micah begins, "you said to be here at—"

"No. It's fine. I told them not to bother me, but according to them, it was an emergency."

Damon casually stands near the lit fireplace as Micah takes in the floor-to-ceiling windows overlooking the breathtakingly beautiful city.

"Can I offer you a tour?" Damon's voice reverts to the calm and collected version he is familiar with.

"It's fine. Only need to know where to sit, eat, bang, and piss." Micah throws pleasantries out the window. After all, this isn't a date, it's a transaction.

"Fair enough. Well, this is where I like to sit. There is the dining room if you'd like a more formal sit down. But I figured to drink and talk, this is the best place."

Micah follows Damon as he begins to lead them through the penthouse. It's not necessarily a tour as he isn't stepping inside each room, but Damon still points out what is behind each door they pass.

"Bathroom is down the hall to the left, at the very end is my bedroom, which you'll see later." A wink is thrown his way. "Here is the kitchen, dining is through that walkway, theatre room is behind the kitchen through that door. Games room is upstairs along with my library and a spare bedroom for when family visits."

"Games room? Library?" Micah sits on the bar stool at the kitchen countertop, feeling out of place amongst such a lavish lifestyle.

"Pool table, gaming consoles, and I believe there is even a Pac-man arcade machine. I'm not sure, I barely use it."

That all sounds great, but it's the library that spikes Micah's interest. He would love to explore it if he's allowed such a privilege. He doesn't recall reading anything about leisurely time in their contract. He takes a deep breath to steady his nerves, suddenly taking in the aroma of the kitchen, the smell making his mouth salivate.

"What smells so good?"

Damon beams. "You'll see. It shouldn't be too much longer. Wine okay?"

"Ahh, I guess. More of a brown liquor kind of guy."

"I figured, but trust me, the red will complement the meal much better."

Damon places a half-filled glass of blood-coloured alcohol in front of him and begins to dish up plates. Micah cautiously takes a sip and *wow, okay,* that is better than any boxed wine he used to steal from his mother.

"Smooth, isn't it," Damon comments.

"Oh, yeah."

"Ought to be, it's a hundred and fifty dollars a bottle."

He almost spits out what's in his mouth until he realises that would be a waste of ten dollars.

With two plates in hand, Damon walks to the small dining table opposite the kitchen countertop where Micah is sitting and places the meals down. He moves to the new location, feeling awkward since this is the first time he's sat across from someone to eat.

Relax. This isn't a date.

His plate contains four thin strips of what looks to be tender, medium rare wagyu beef, and the only reason he knows what that looks like is because the owner of the bookstore always has cooking channels on in the background while she sits behind the counter with her small portable TV.

Beside it sits chargrilled asparagus, some whole carrots and a few baby potatoes—a light enough meal before any bedroom activity.

"The asparagus has a vinaigrette on it, and the carrots are honey-coated. A light seasoning of rosemary and salt on the potatoes, and the beef, you can eat as is or I made a red wine jus."

"This is…not what I was expecting." His knife cuts through the meat like butter, and it isn't even a steak knife.

"One of the biggest misconceptions about gays is that we can eat anything before sex," Damon states. "Sex on a full stomach is hard enough, feeling the weight in my abdomen, the risk of getting a stitch or being gassy. But *being* fucked, no guy wants a dick up his ass after eating a greasy burger and fries."

Micah laughs a real, honest-to-God laugh. Something he didn't think he'd do in the presence of this man.

"You're not wrong there." Micah thinks about how well he cleaned himself before coming over this evening. That process takes time and effort, which would have been ruined within twenty minutes of finishing a meal such as the one described.

"Besides," Damon continues, still chuckling at his joke. "I love to cook. It's how I spend my free time."

"You have a lot of that?" Micah asks. "You know, free time." He bites into an asparagus, surprised at how sweet it tastes.

"Hmm, on and off. A lot of my work I do from home since I'm more behind the scenes. Besides, cooking allows me to once again provide for someone, make sure they are eating well, and taking care of their bodies."

"I knew it." He shoves another potato in his mouth, chews, and only then does he continue. "You're a drug dealer, aren't you?"

Damon puts his cutlery down, intrigued by the comment. "What makes you think that?"

"You're thirty-five and have all of this." He gestures around the room with his knife. "You work behind the scenes, which means you have nobodies like me dealing for you. And you're into the whole Dom punishment, power trip thing, so…" Micah doesn't care if Damon *is* a drug dealer. Again, they aren't dating, but it would be nice to know if Damon's rival might come for him, thinking that they could get a one-up on him if they killed the guy's fuck toy.

Wait. Is he a fuck toy?

"Interesting analysis of my life, but no, Micah. I'm not a dealer."

"No one's going to come after me then?"

"I sure hope not. We haven't even started yet, but I do plan on keeping you around."

Unsure how to process that comment, he moves along. "Okay, Mr Confident, what's your deal then?"

"Truth?"

"Obviously."

"I inherited it from my mentor."

Tonight seems to be a night of the unexpected.

"Like a sugar daddy?"

"Not so crude, but I suppose so."

"And now the tables have turned and you're the one into younger guys."

"Micah, I'm not that much older than you," Damon states before explaining further. "I found myself at a young age dabbling in the BDSM world before I knew enough about it to be safe."

Micah sits up straight, giving his full attention.

"Mistakes were made and after a bad experience where I found myself in what's called a Dom drop, I was approached by a Dominant who offered to teach me how to be a true Dom. A respectable, caring, giving, and nurturing human being that could give demands, discipline and punishment in a safe environment."

"So, what, he Dommed you?"

"Yes."

Micah's surprised.

"The best way to learn is by doing. It just so happened that he was verse, which worked in my favour, but still, bottoms can be in control, as I'm sure you're aware."

Micah reaches for his wine, needing a gulp or two to take the edge off.

"He taught me everything I know. He allowed me to play with others once he thought I was ready and sometimes watched, but I would still come back to him, ask questions or dominate him for practice here and there." Damon picks up his wine glass but does not yet have a drink.

"He passed away unexpectedly, and it was only then that I learnt of the changes he made to his will, leaving me the small fortune he made throughout his career."

There are two very important key factors that he needs to remind himself of. One, this relationship of sorts is in the past, and two, the guy is dead. It's important because Damon's history is painting visuals in Micah's mind that seem to be awakening a little green monster inside of him. Jealousy.

"Wow. You honestly had no idea?"

"None. I was twenty-four."

"Jesus…"

"As I said, I got into this world young. A confused kid with no one to help guide me."

The version of Damon he initially had in his mind is vastly changing the more he learns. "What do you do now?"

"Well, money doesn't last forever, no matter how much you have. I decided to become a silent investor in the club where I met my Dom. Over time, I came across more clubs that had potential but needed investors, clubs that were willing to listen to my opinion, hear my ideas." Damon takes a sip of his wine and then puts his glass down. "My latest endeavour is the club you frequent."

"Really?" He's surprised. Being that it's one of the best, he figures Damon would have started there.

"Of course. I've been visiting that club for two years. I know how everything works, which means I can see its flaws."

"What's taking so long?"

"Well, the owner is, how should I put it, *traditional*, perhaps. He believes the only people that should be investing in his club are those committed."

"Committed? As in, to their roles?"

"Their roles and their relationships. He has had his Sub for thirty-two years. She's collared, owned, and he figures anyone who *plays* in that role is merely dipping their toes into the world, so to speak."

"So, what, you need to find a Sub and only be with them to be taken seriously? What about those pompous people you were talking about?"

"Polyamorous? He doesn't believe in such a thing."

"Traditional or bigot?"

"It's fine. I'm sure I'll eventually persuade him. Perhaps once he realises that the clubs beginning to catch up to him are all owned by me, he'll see no other choice."

"I thought you said you were only an investor."

"I mean, at first I was, but eventually I bought more shares until I had the majority." Damon winks, picking his cutlery back up.

They both finish eating and Micah is surprised by how easy it is to sit down and enjoy a meal with Damon. The only part of this transaction he thought he'd struggle with. Well, this and pretending to be a Little. But that's a whole other situation.

When they move to the living room and sit on the couch opposite the fireplace, Micah finds himself telling Damon about his job, who instantly offers to show him the library upstairs whenever he wants to see it. Micah speaks about how he hopes to one day take over the business when the current owner retires. He shares his plans to make it into a store for boutique authors, the ones not published by the big names that are killing the market for the little guys.

As he speaks, Damon reaches out and gently caresses his cheek. Micah isn't used to such a tender touch and flinches on instinct.

"I'm sorry. Forgive me. I should have asked."

"No, no. That's not—it was just a caress. Not like you were shoving your tongue down my throat."

"All contact should be consensual, Micah. Sexual or otherwise. It was wrong of me. I hope you can forgive me."

Micah rolls his eyes, "Relax. Here." To prove not only to himself but also to Damon that he is fine with the touch, Micah takes Damon's hand and places his palm directly on his cheek.

His cheek fits perfectly in the palm of Damon's hand, a fact which is comforting in a way Micah can't understand. As Damon's thumb begins to rub under his cheekbone, he can't help but lean into the touch.

"What do you want tonight, Micah?"

"I thought Friday was about—" Damon's chuckle cuts him off.

"No, I mean, tell me *how* you want it?"

He gulps. "I want it…I want it hard."

"Mhm. I kind of figured. What else?" His cheek is still being caressed. He catches the way Damon's green eyes flick down to look at his lips before they lock back on him.

"I don't…I mean…I'm not used to…"

"How about I tell you what I'd like to do, and you let me know if you'd like that or not?"

He nods.

Why does he feel like this is his first time?

Something about Damon makes him nervous. Not scared, just elated.

"I want to eat you out."

"*Fuck.*" The word falls from his mouth like a whispered promise.

"Has anyone done that to you before?"

"I mean…not worthy of remembering."

Damon growls. "I promise, you'll remember me…" His voice drops. It's deep and seductive. "You'll remember the way my tongue opens you up. You'll remember the way I tease you. Ravish you. Nibble at your flesh. I want to eat you out until you come. Then, once I bury my fingers inside of you, making sure you're stretched enough to take me—because I can assure you, there's a lot to take—*then* I will fuck you within an inch of your life."

Micah's dick is already straining against his jeans, and Damon hasn't even touched him. "Ye-yeah. Yeah, I want that."

Since they shared their test results three days prior, Micah's been daydreaming of experiencing that sensation of skin on skin. Of being filled during *and* after the sex. Damon stands from the couch and offers his hand, which Micah obligingly takes before he follows the brunet down the hallway to the room at the end, just like he promised.

The decor of Damon's bedroom matches his personality. With its neutral tones of whites, greys, and the occasional black. The only pops of colour come from a plant here and there, artistic photos on the walls, and the lights of the city that can be seen from the balcony.

In the middle of the room is a four-post wooden frame bed. In the corner near the window sits what looks to be a chair of some sort, though its weird arch makes him question whether it's something that should be in a therapist's office.

"Wow, how very *Ideal Home*," Micah teases. "Where's all the fifty shades? The red room of pain?" Damon pulls out a drawer that is hidden under the bed, as wide as the super king mattress, revealing an array of butt plugs, dildos, prostate massagers, floggers, paddles, whips, canes, cuffs, rope, cock rings, ball gags, vibrators and more.

Micah can't deny some of it looks daunting, while certain toys spike his interest.

"It's all new. I never play with toys I've used on others. And if we never play with any of it, then that's okay also. But I wanted you to know that it's there."

Damon pushes the drawer back in. Micah's only familiar with a paddle or flogger from playing at the club, though many of the other toys are ones he has seen before. He finally bought his first dildo after moving out. His mother had a habit of searching his room, and no amount of pleasure was worth the risk of her finding it. He isn't opposed to trying a few, but not tonight. Not for his first time with Damon.

He's brought out of his head as Damon walks towards him.

"I'm going to start touching you now, is that okay?"

"For the love of God, yes already." He gets a small thrill saying the *g* word when he's about to partake in a cardinal sin. It feels powerful. Like he's getting something back that was taken from him. That was never his belief, merely that of his parents, who forced it upon him. What he believes in is letting the man before him satisfy every dirty desire.

Damon lays his hands upon Micah's biceps, the touch relaxing him instantly.

"What are the colours, Micah?"

"Seriously? We're only having sex."

"Sometimes sex can go beyond a person's boundaries. Safety is the priority, even before pleasure."

He groans in frustration. "Green, good to go. Yellow, slow the hell down. Red, stop or I'll knock you out."

"And what are you now?" Damon questions.

"Green, of course."

A hand moves from his bicep, back to his cheek. He inhales right before Damon's lips land on his.

The cliché of fireworks erupting when Damon captures his lips is an understatement. His body ignites with a fire he has never felt in his entire life. He wants to inform Damon that he doesn't generally kiss but at this stage, he wonders why he had such a rule. Micah sinks into the kiss. Damon's hand holds his cheek firm while the other slips down to his waist, so their bodies are pressed together tightly.

He moans, embarrassed by the sound when it's merely a kiss, but it allows for his lips to open, a sign Damon takes as permission to slide his tongue inside, which tastes better than the meal they shared.

It's Damon who breaks the kiss, but not the contact. Their foreheads rest against one another as Micah's chest expands with each lungful of air. Fingers play with the hair at the nape of Micah's neck, soothing him and keeping him grounded as his mind battles with itself. A kiss should not be this intense.

"Micah?" Damon whispers. "Would you hold it against me if I said that no kiss has ever felt like that before?"

"You're just saying that." He tells himself it's all part of the wooing process of a Dom. *Right?*

"No…" Damon shakes his head as he pulls back, their eyes locking on one another. "As I promised you; I never lie."

Micah swallows, his eyes dropping to Damon's swollen pink lips, and he wants more. Damon seems to catch on and leans back in, only this time, as their mouths attach and try to connect as one entity, their hands begin to roam, undoing buttons and kicking off shoes.

It's messy, and not at all graceful, but the second Micah is topless, his back pressed to the mattress, it seems to awaken something within Damon.

Damon stands tall, looking down at him, eyes roaming his body and it makes him feel self-conscious. His body has never been looked at for longer than it takes to find his hole or his dick. However, the look on Damon's face has Micah suddenly feeling empowered. He may be the one who is about to be devoured, but he can see in Damon's eyes that if he so much as whispers the words 'wait' or 'slow down', Damon will obey like a trained dog.

Micah unzips his jeans and shimmies out of them as gracefully as he can in his position. He throws them on the floor, not caring where they land, eyes still locked on Damon's. Not wanting to wait any longer, he turns around and gets on his hands and knees.

"*God*, Micah. I knew your ass was something special, but seeing it like this, being presented to me." Damon runs a hand from Micah's tailbone up to the base of his neck where it grips him firmly. Micah holds his breath as wet lips linger near his ear.

"I told you," Damon whispers. "Your body is already submitting to me without you even knowing." He bites his ear. "It's what you crave."

Micah whines. A sound he isn't familiar with emitting.

"Colour?" Damon checks.

"Green." And just like that, giant hands knead into the flesh of his ass and spread his cheeks open. Moments later, the warmth of Damon's tongue dives in without any warning.

One of the aspects of himself, besides his sexuality, that defied his parents and their beliefs was Micah's filthy mouth. Not a single care for what came out or who heard it. But nothing he's ever said in the past could compare to the profanity he spills as Damon ravishes his ass. The man's tongue did wonders in his mouth, but the things it is doing to his rim, he's never experienced anything like it.

What starts as kitten licks slowly increases in length and pressure. Damon works his way from his balls to his rim; his tongue is the brush and Micah's ass is the canvas, and he's sure if he could see it, the painting would be incredible. Teeth graze his flesh, but they never bite down, as much as he wants them to.

Cold air suddenly lands on his wet skin and it has him quivering. He's about to complain about the sudden stop in pleasure when spit hits him like an arrow getting a bullseye. Damon goes back in, circling his pink ring of muscles that Micah can feel loosening, granting deeper access.

Time is lost, as is the strength in Micah's arms. Unable to hold himself up, his chest crashes to the mattress, tilting his ass higher in the air.

"Your hole is so needy, clenching around my tongue." Damon acts like a starved man whose favourite meal has been placed in front of him.

The noises are like a filthy symphony. Sweat drips down Micah's spine and pools at his neck, the pain of his release begging to be let go. Micah knows he has to find his voice and speak up.

"I—Damon," he strains.

"Colour?" He suspects Damon takes the struggle in his voice as a bad thing.

"Green, but it won't be unless you let me come."

"Why Micah, all you had to do was ask." Damon's index finger slides inside of him without any resistance and as it massages his prostate, Micah shoots warm, thick strings of cum onto the bedding. He's sure whoever lives beneath Damon can hear his earth-shattering moans.

"That's it, Micah. Just relax. You did *so good* letting me eat you out," Damon coos as Micah shudders through his release.

His legs are slowly being pulled out so he's lying flat on the mattress. The hands that were spreading him open now rub his thighs, easing his muscles.

"Would you like to stop, Micah?" He's taken aback by Damon's question.

"You don't wanna fuck?" Micah rolls over, finding whatever energy he can to lean on his elbows, eyes focusing on how hard Damon is straining in his pants.

"Trust me, there is nothing I want more. But if that was too much, I can wait."

Cocking an eyebrow, it occurs to him that Damon is willing to give himself blue balls, and once again, his words echo in his ear;

"I want to put your needs before my own." Micah didn't believe that meant he would get off and Damon wouldn't.

"You promised to fuck me so hard I can't walk. Don't tell me you're all talk." Micah bites his lip, giving Damon his answer with whatever sarcasm he can muster.

The brunet unbuckles his belt, the sound of it being pulled through the loops sends a tremble through Micah's body. He isn't ashamed to admit that the second Damon's pants are off, his eyes fall to his dick, which results in his mouth hanging open like a goldfish.

"Didn't your mother ever teach you that it's rude to gawk? You don't close that mouth, Micah, I may just have to fill it."

The sound of his teeth connecting as he snaps his mouth closed makes Damon smirk.

"Good boy."

Micah melts.

There is a hunger in Damon as he crawls up the mattress, his muscular body hovers over Micah's who isn't used to seeing his sexual conquests up close and personal.

"Don't you dare think for a second you're rolling over for this," Damon states.

He swallows. "Not really used to it any other way."

Damon's hand rests on his face, his thumb once again strokes his cheek. Micah's starting to suspect this is Damon's way of using action over verbal cues. A way to settle the energy inside of him.

"I wouldn't dream of not being able to see your face the first time I push inside that sweet, puffy, pink hole of yours."

He's only slightly embarrassed at how Damon's words have his legs falling open a little wider.

He waits, eyes locked on Damon's. His heart begins to beat in sync with the man above him, whose chest is pressed against his.

Micah holds his breath. He feels the tip of the delicious, nine-inch uncut dick press against his rim.

He swallows.

The second Damon pushes inside enough for Micah to feel himself stretch around the biggest dick he's ever taken, his head tilts back, his eyes close and his mouth falls open into the perfect O.

"*Micah…*"

The way his name falls from Damon's lips, it's almost like a command, causing Micah's head to snap up, green eyes meeting hazel as Damon thrusts his hips at an agonisingly slow pace. It seems to be what Damon wants; but once their eyes lock, his pace begins to quicken. Micah loves the way he can feel Damon slide against his walls, the rawness adding to the mind-blowing sensation of being fucked open until he is nothing more than a gaping hole.

"Give it to me, Damon. Prove you're the Daddy you say you are."

Like a wind-up monkey that plays the symbols, Damon is suddenly at full force. By saying *that* word, calling him *that* name, it awakens something inside of him

Damon sits back on his heels, grips Micah's legs and holds them up in a wide V, pounding so hard that Micah's head keeps hitting the bed frame. Micah couldn't care less. His ass is sucking Damon in deep and holding on tight as he tries to slide out.

To his surprise, when calling Damon 'Daddy', it didn't cause his skin to crawl or his dick to go soft the way he thought it would. It has, however, boosted Damon's confidence in a way he didn't expect the brunet to need.

He tries again. "Give it to me, Daddy. Fill me up."

"Jesus, fuck. *Micah.*" Damon loses it the second he says those words. The warmth of Damon's cum shooting inside of him; he's never felt anything as heavenly. Damon's thrusts aren't slowing, pushing his cum deeper and deeper. Micah's legs are being pulled higher, so his ass lifts off the mattress, as though Damon doesn't want a single drop to leak out of him.

Micah's lost in the way Damon's eyes are zeroing in on his dick as it slowly slides in and out of Micah's ass, coated in his cum, playing with it. They both groan from the sensation. Like watching their own personal porn video. Micah's legs return to the mattress once Damon's gone soft and can no longer slip into the warmth of his hole.

Whether it's because his drought is finally over or the realisation that he'll be seeing Damon tomorrow, the next day and possibly the following week has seeped into his mind, Micah's calm afterglow suddenly fades as his typical desire to make like the wind and vanish kicks in.

"That was…you sure weren't lying." Micah rolls to the side, avoiding the panting body beside him as he leans over to find his clothes, wincing a little from the ache in his ass and the ooze of cum that leaks out of him.

"Thanks…"

He can hear the trepidation in Damon's voice.

Forgoing his underwear, he slips on his jeans, realising his mistake when a wet patch instantly appears on the denim as he zips and buttons up.

"You know you don't have to leave. I figured since I'll be seeing you tomorrow that—"

"All good. Didn't pack for a sleepover."

Damon leans on his elbow. "You can borrow from me."

"'S fine. Better be getting back." He shoves his shirt on, only buttoning a few buttons to make the process quicker.

"Same time tomorrow, I guess?"

He finally meets Damon's eyes. "Sure…yeah…ah, thanks."

He hobbles towards the elevator, wishing he could bask in the beautiful ache and throb of his ass. His body protests each step he takes as he gets a twinge in his lower back.

The second he sits in his car, it's as though he's sat in a pool of slime. He loves it. He rolls his hips a little, feeling the cum stick to his cheeks, some areas already hard and rubbing against his jeans. He's never fucked raw before, but he is a slut for how turned on he is by the sensation.

He ignores the voices in his head telling him he should have stayed, that he didn't have to run. He especially ignores the loud, obnoxious threats in his head that tell him he ruined something good.

As he climbs up to his third-floor studio apartment, the one that now feels like a prison cell after being in the wide-open space of Damon's penthouse, his phone dings and he knows in his heart who it is without looking, and yet he still does.

Damon

> I hope you're okay.

> You ran out so fast I didn't get a chance to ask, which has left me feeling somewhat troubled.

> I told you aftercare is non-negotiable, Micah. It's needed just as much for me as it is for you.

He feels the cum drip down his leg as he types out his answer.

Micah

> It was just sex. Why the hell do I need aftercare?

Why is he being so hostile?

If not for the three dancing dots, he would be panicking about how long Damon's reply takes.

> The mind is incredibly vulnerable after sex, and aftercare maintains respect between those involved. It safeguards the emotional safety and security of both partners. After such a high-intensity moment, we need a chance to reset, Micah. Aftercare can create a bridge between our intimate world and the one we are a part of the rest of the time. You don't have to be in pain to require the need to feel cared for or for me to show some affection and nurturing tendencies.

That, he wasn't expecting.

> Sorry. Figured it was only for the spanking and shit. Just wanted to come home and crash after a big day.

He bites his lip.

> I'll be sure to stick around long enough for you to do what you need to do tomorrow.

He locks his screen and then opens it again, his fingers working quicker than his mind can tell him not to.

> Thanks for tonight. Really was something else.

Chapter 5
Trial Run; The Spanking

Damon sits in front of the fire, waiting for Micah to arrive. He's on edge. Not sexually, but the way things ended last night left him feeling anxious. He expected there to be some light conversation after sex, maybe a cuddle session or at least a 'How was it for you?' but Micah had run out the door quicker than his dick could stop leaking from the earth-shattering orgasm.

He's been fantasising about Micah's ass since the day he watched the inexperienced man walk into the club and pull his pants down for some unappreciative jerkwad to flog. But that ass, he had no idea the power it held. He felt possessed as he pushed inside, feeling Micah clench around him. He had to jerk off this morning after he lay in bed thinking about it and again not too long before he got ready for the evening.

The elevator doors open, and Damon quickly adjusts himself as Micah steps into the room. He takes in Micah's hesitancy, something he didn't expect after their encounter the night before.

"Hello, again." He smiles at Micah, which seems to relax the younger man.

"Hey. I, um, I wasn't sure what I'd be walking into to be perfectly honest."

Damon tilts his head. "You thought I'd be angry?"

Micah shrugs. "Your text seemed—"

"Hurt. Confused," he cuts Micah off. "I recall at our meeting that you said you were more of a, shall I say, one-and-done kind of guy, but per our agreement, I thought I'd at least get to shower before you walked out the door."

Micah bites his bottom lip and by God, he wants to bite it for him. So. Fucking. Bad.

"Have you eaten?" Damon asks

"Yeah. Friday is dinner, remember."

"Of course." *That doesn't mean he doesn't wish to share more dinners with him.*

People are what Damon knows. He can read their bodies and social cues. He can sometimes understand them better than themselves. There are parts of Micah he has pieced together, but mostly, he is an enigma, and all Damon wants to do is solve him.

"Follow me." Damon drops the tone of his voice, slipping into his role since Micah seems to be ready to play. It feels so familiar to assert himself in this position. It's natural to him, almost more so than being Damon Stone. It's a second skin that has his heart racing with adrenalin and his hands tingling for skin-on-skin spanking.

He can't help but smirk at the way Micah stands up straighter, holding his shoulders firm as the younger man begins to walk towards him, following him to the bedroom.

Once inside, Damon closes the door and begins to roll the sleeves of his black button-up shirt to his elbow.

"You came to the club looking for pain, for a release," Damon states. "For this, I don't know why, and unless you wish to share, I don't need to know." He begins to roll up his other sleeve. "What I do know is, you looked at the biggest instrument in the club and thought that would be what you needed. But that's not always the case." He finishes and looks over at Micah who seems to be on edge, perhaps with nerves, excitement, maybe a little hesitancy.

He steps towards him, his hands casually in his pockets as he walks around his new toy.

"We ask for pain as it may facilitate a reprieve or escape from the burdensome responsibilities of adulthood. Forgive me if I've overstepped, but I sense your desire for pain stems more from the built-up frustrations of your parents...their beliefs."

"What are you going on about? I'm not here to chit-chat."

"Nor am I, Micah." He walks back towards the bed and takes a seat, his legs spread open as he rests his elbows on his knees.

"When we don't have control of our lives, we lash out at others or seek out that which we can gain control of. Spanking is your pain to help quiet your mind. To help shut down the voices of the past while having control over what level of pain you're enduring."

He studies Micah's face, making sure he's taking in every single word.

"Submissives have the control, Micah. *Always.* When you walked into that club asking for what you wanted, you were in control. When you stood up, no longer wanting any further punishment, you. Were. In. Control."

Damon sits up straight. "Bare-hand spanking offers feedback to the spanker. When using a bare hand, you can feel how hard you're hitting someone. It offers a level of intimacy through skin-on-skin contact and most of all, it can bruise and leave you feeling tender for days without having to break the skin like other spanking toys can do."

Taking in a deep breath, he slowly releases it, feeling himself sink deeper into the role of Dom Daddy. This is who he is. Who he was born to be. This is what Damon loves and as he opens his eyes, gazing at Micah, he feels a hunger that he hasn't felt with anyone else before.

"Drop your pants," he commands. "Lay over my knee." He wants to recreate the way they were positioned the first time he was privileged to touch that gorgeous pillowy-soft ass. He has many ideas for what he hopes will be next time, especially with his tantra chair he noticed Micah eyeing off last night.

Micah lays over his lap. He's made sure to sit far back enough on the mattress so that Micah's hands can rest on the bed rather than have his head hang low and risk the blood rushing down.

"What's your colour, Micah?"

"Green."

"And how hard do you want it?"

There is a pause, a sign that Micah is considering his answer, which he is proud to see.

"When I sit down tomorrow, I want to be able to remember why it hurts."

Damon knows exactly how far to go.

"I'm going to start with ten to each cheek."

His flat palm makes contact, and the sound echoes in his room. He glances at Micah, whose eyes are closed. His face seems to have softened, even though it is only the first hit.

Damon continues. Nine more smacks to the left cheek, keeping his palm firm and focused on the one area that has already coloured to a hot pink tinge. The sight is glorious. The bounce of Micah's ass is mouth-watering, but Damon's attention stays on his hand technique as he calculates each spank.

Before he moves to the next cheek, he checks in while rubbing his hand against the beaten skin. "Colour?"

"Green." Micah's voice sounds relaxed.

Moving forward, he applies ten firm slaps to Micah's right cheek.

The reason he prefers bare-hand spanking to instruments is because the level of pain doesn't necessarily come from the impact, though that does largely come into play. It more so comes from the speed of the slap.

Quick spanks lead to a fast series of sharp pains, not giving the spankee a chance to process one hit before the next one strikes. If he spaces them out, going a little slower like he is now, it gives Micah a chance to take in every sensation, including the feel of Damon's hand pressing against his cheek.

If asked for a whip, a flogger or even a paddle, he would offer it, but this is his chance to prove he understands what Micah needs, and that it isn't from anything more than human touch.

At the end of the ten, he once again rubs his palm gently over the reddened skin.

"How are you feeling?"

"Warm."

He smiles. It seems Micah is somewhat of a brat. It's endearing. In the past, his play partners were either compliant or downright spiteful. They inhabited a role that they thought he wanted from them, but Micah, he's playful. Brats like to be rebellious; they like to misbehave and disobey to make their Dominants work for the Submissive side. They are cheeky and he can see that in Micah, though he isn't sure if the younger man realises this is what he's doing. Micah's smart-ass remarks have him fighting back verbally and he suspects in the future his little brat may do so physically too. He can't wait, knowing the reward of getting Micah to behave will be worth it.

For round two, Damon goes for a cupped hand technique. It naturally gives off a louder sound, which causes Micah to jump, knowing that in terms of impact, the feeling isn't that different to a flat palm. But what he loves about a cupped hand is how beautifully it marks the skin. Damon aims more for the lower cheek, alternating from left to right. With each smack, he sinks further into his role. His pleasure comes from how well Micah is responding to his techniques, and that's enough for him.

In life, there are three basic human pleasures: food, sex, and giving. He fed Micah yesterday and the sex between them was a sensation overload. Now, he is giving, and although his dick is soft, it's still a euphoric feeling that he could bask in for eternity.

This time around, he doesn't stop at ten smacks. Instead, he waits until Micah is squirming on his lap. It's then that he rubs the hot-to-touch skin, soothing his hand and Micah's ass simultaneously.

"Colour?"

"Mmm, green." Micah is leaning on his elbows, his forehead resting on his hands, which are interlocked.

"One more round for tonight," Damon explains. He told Micah he is in control of when he starts and stops, and he meant it, but it's his duty as the Dominant to know when to stop in case his Sub is trying to push himself too far. He has seen Micah try to take more than he can handle simply to prove something, whether it be to himself or, Damon suspects, his parents. He doesn't want to push Micah to a point where he doesn't return, but he does want to prove that he can give Micah what he's been seeking.

His hand slaps against the gloriously red cheek in a swiping motion, from his lower cheek up toward his lower back, though his hand never makes impact outside of the cushioned tooshie.

"Ah, fuck," Micah lets out.

"Colour?"

"Gr—yellow."

"Let's take a moment."

"No!" Micah barks.

"*Micah...*" He's stern.

"I'm fine. Just wasn't expecting such a sting."

He rubs soothing circles into Micah's flesh. "That's what this technique is best for."

"God, it felt good," Micah huffs.

"Want me to continue?"

"Yeah. Please." Micah turns his face, so he is looking directly at him. "Promise, I'm green."

He believes him. This technique can pack a punch, but after the beating Micah's ass has taken, it would no doubt feel three times as powerful. He decides ten to each cheek will be enough.

With every swipe up, he can see the imprint of his hand on both cheeks, not yet faded before the next spank lands.

As he counts down in his head, he drags each spank out a little further apart, helping with the sting between each hit.

He, too, tries not to get lost in the power. He studies Micah's face and analyses his body. Between each spank, he watches.

Does Micah flinch? Does he tense? Does he jerk away in anticipation of each smack? By the time he reaches ten, Micah is panting. Pliant. Damon couldn't be prouder.

He continues to gently rub the skin, waiting for the adrenaline to settle within himself before he asks Micah to stand.

"Good boy, Micah. You handled that spanking so well. I couldn't be more in awe."

Damon's not hard. As arousing as the sight is, he's trained his body to behave. The ability to control himself has left some partners confused, wondering why he isn't rock hard from their scene together. However, this isn't sexual to him. Though it can be used sexually, he understands the difference. Micah, too, is soft. This is a different type of release for him, and he can see in Micah's posture and face that he's helped the beautiful young man achieve it.

"I'm going to move you to the bed, okay? I don't want you to stand just yet." Micah offers a nod and with that, Damon slides his relaxed partner off his lap as though Micah weighs nothing at all, slipping himself off the mattress as he moves his delicate beauty further up the bed. He watches the subdued man wrap his arms around one of his pillows, and whether it is a coincidence or not, it's the one Damon sleeps on every night, the one that would most likely have a scent to it…his scent.

In the bathroom, he retrieves a cooling gel, one that will soothe the heat without taking away the ache. When he returns, Micah's eyes have drifted closed, but his breathing indicates that he's not yet asleep.

"Micah?" he asks softly, as if he were talking to a tired child.

"Mhm."

"I'm going to apply some gel, okay?"

"But I 'ike da 'ain" Micah mumbles against the pillow.

"You'll still have the pain, just going to take some of the heat off to balance your temperature.

"Wa'ever"

Damon chuckles, shaking his head at the adorable behaviour. Gently, he applies the cooling gel, the clear liquid causing a hiss to fall from the lips of his new play partner the second it hits the skin.

"Shhh, there you go." He rubs the tender skin. "Your ass has some pretty marks, Micah." He applies a thick layer to the other cheek. He's about to leave to clean off his hand when the words slip from a sleepy yet coherent mouth.

"Thank you, Daddy."

Proud.

That's how Damon feels. He gave Micah what he's been chasing, for who knows how long, whether it's been months or years, but Damon's made him feel safe and special, which is all he wants for Micah. Damon kneels beside the bed, his clean hand reaching out to run his fingers through slicked-back hair.

"You can stay as long as you need, Micah. You don't have to run off. You're safe. Enjoy the moment. Can you do that, please? For me?"

Soft eyes flutter open, and Damon has to stop himself from gasping at how much younger Micah suddenly looks. The hardness in those hazel eyes has seeped away, leaving behind this tender vulnerability that he suspects has been hidden for over a decade.

"You going to be mad if I go?" Micah asks.

"No." His fingers are still running through Micah's hair. "But I would be concerned about you driving home like this. I'd have to insist on driving you, walk you to your door."

"Fucking Doms, always needing to be in control of everything."

He chuckles softly so as not to disturb Micah's zen-like space.

"Fine," Micah huffs. "I'll stay." Damon keeps his smile at bay, though it would go from ear to ear if he allowed himself to show it. The beautiful treasure closes his eyes again, a sign that the conversation is over.

In the bathroom, he cleans off his hand but keeps the gel beside the bed in case Micah needs it during the night. He takes a moment to bask in his own afterglow. That deep, powerful sensation of being in control. A restraint on himself, his life, and dare he hope, his Sub. The anxious feeling he had before Micah's arrival has simmered down to a quiet hum, a white noise that soothes him to the point of drowsiness. But that could also be from reaching his desired space, much like Micah had while being spanked.

With a final deep breath in and out, he steps back into the role of Damon and quietly retrieves a glass of water from the kitchen for his play partner, placing it on the nightstand. Changing into a pair of night pants and forgoing a top like he does every other night, he glances at Micah's sleeping form, aware that he is naked from the waist down. He covers him with a warm, faux fur throw blanket. The texture would feel like silk on his red-hot buttocks.

Sliding under the duvet, he switches off the light and falls asleep to the soft purring snores coming from the man beside him.

It's their first time playing together and yet, Damon is absolutely hooked. All he can hope is that Micah is also getting the same vibe from their experiences and will be happy to continue with a permanent contract. He's aware that tomorrow, however, will be the big decider for Micah, which is why Damon spent all of today putting everything together to make it perfect for him.

Chapter 6
The Trial Run; The Little

RACHEL O'ROURKE

When Micah wakes, it takes him a moment to remember where he is as he catches sight of the city landscape from the large windows in front of him, the balcony bright as the sun's rays reflect off the glass.

He is still in his shirt from the night before, still naked from the waist down and as he turns to see if Damon is beside him, he hisses in delight as his skin pulls and sends an ache to his ass cheeks.

It's perfect.

The bed is empty and although he's a little disappointed, he's also relieved, unsure of what the protocol is when waking up beside a guy who not only fucked him good but then whooped his ass until he was putty in the older man's hands.

He turns back and notices a glass of water on the bedside table, along with what he assumes is Advil. Beside the glass is a note:

Sweatpants are in the bathroom for you.
Feel free to shower, otherwise, breakfast is ready.
Daddy

He swallows the pills dry and then downs the glass of water. Last night's activities don't affect his walk, but as he bends to slip the soft cashmere sweatpants over his legs, he feels the tenderness of his ass.

He smiles. He's relaxed. His mind is quiet for the first time in…forever.

Out in the kitchen, Damon is putting the last of what looks to be scrambled eggs onto a plate. Micah tries not to drool at the sight of Damon's ass hugged beautifully in grey sweatpants that are no doubt also cashmere. He has a sleep shirt on and looks utterly beautiful.

"Good morning," Damon interrupts his daydreaming. "I wasn't sure if I was going to have to wake you."

Micah rubs at the back of his neck, feeling a little out of sorts, but the growl of his stomach convinces him to get over it.

"Before you sit," Damon begins.

Micah looks up from the food to see Damon holding up soothing gel. "Figured you might need some."

"Ah, ye-yeah. Sure."

Damon walks around the counter. "Can you please turn around for Daddy?"

Micah grumbles, but still does as Damon asks, figuring the quicker he gets it over with the faster he can eat. Damon's warm hand is gentle, which Micah appreciates as his ass twinges the second any pressure is put onto his cheek.

"How are you feeling?" Damon asks.

"Good. I kinda forget it's there until I sit or bend or twist in any way."

Damon lifts Micah's sweatpants away from his cheeks so as not to touch his skin as they are pulled back up.

"Which is, ya know, what I was after." He sits at the small table where he ate dinner two nights before, groaning as he relishes in the discomfort.

Damon places the plate of eggs, bacon, toast, and fruit in front of him, with a glass of orange juice and a mug of coffee.

"If I knew staying over meant this level of service, I might not have left the other night." He tries to joke, not knowing what else to say or do in this situation.

"Don't flatter yourself. I would have cooked the same for myself even if you weren't here."

Micah cocks an eyebrow in question.

"I'm serious, Micah. Healthy body, healthy mind. Need it to be able to think clearly if I'm going to be spanking that sweet, sweet tooshie of yours."

"Ugh, don't say tooshie." He shoves his mouth full of food.

"Buttocks?"

"No."

"Booty."

"Jesus."

"Gluteus maximus"

"I swear to God."

Damon is laughing at this point. "Fine, fine. I'll stop." Damon takes a sip of his coffee, which looks to be as black as his. Good. He doesn't trust anyone who adds creams and milk to their coffee. Sugar, have at it.

"I will say though, I very much enjoyed last night. So, thank you, for trusting me with that opportunity."

It's weird. No one has ever thanked Micah for pommelling his ass before. But as he shoves more food in his mouth to prevent himself from saying something obnoxious, he kind of likes the feeling of holding that power. Of having someone thank him for doing *him* a service.

He doesn't mention the moment from last night where *he* thanked Damon, nor the fact that the word Daddy slipped from his lips once again and so easily.

They finish eating and as Micah chugs the glass of juice, Damon wipes his mouth with a cloth napkin and stands from the table.

"I guess it's time to show you your surprise."

Micah rolls his eyes. He knows what today is, what's expected of him, so he isn't sure why Damon is calling it a surprise. As he trudges behind Damon, it occurs to him that the sex and the spanking have both been better than anything he's experienced in his life, which is saying something. Perhaps this contract might not be so bad. He wonders if he can negotiate for none of this Little crap once he's done for the day, focusing purely on getting that delicious nine inches and those giant, firm hands.

They stop at the door to the right, opposite the bathroom, before Damon's bedroom at the end of the hall.

"This room is for you," Damon says as he places his hand on the door handle.

"For me?" He's confused.

"This is your space every Sunday. If you wish for Daddy to join you, you must give permission, otherwise, I cannot enter this room. It's only for Michelangelo." Damon opens the door, but Micah is caught off guard by the use of his full name, unable to take in what's before him.

He blinks a couple of times and then focuses. The room is bright, refreshing, with a clean forest-type smell to it. The walls are painted a soft baby blue. Without really looking, they'd almost seem white, as though the blue is an illusion, a trick of the eye. The room also has a balcony; there must be one in every bedroom. On it, Micah can see a small plastic blow-up pool, big enough for a couple of kids or what he assumes, one adult.

Within the pastel blue walls, there is a huge bean bag that seems large enough for three adults. Its grey material looks fluffy and soft, reminding Micah of the blanket Damon had draped over him the night before.

There is a small wooden table and chairs in a corner. Micah walks over towards it, unaware he had stepped foot inside the room. His eyes catch the adult colouring books. He picks one up and flips through the pages, which feature cartoon drawings of dicks, and one has the middle finger with flower vines wrapping around the hand. There are pages of spanked bums and men tied in rope. It is hot and somewhat erotic once Micah looks past the elements that give it that colouring book vibe.

He chucks it back down and spots a TV on one of the walls, one much larger than any he has ever owned.

"It's connected to Disney+ and Netflix Kids. Nothing higher than a PG rating. Though maybe if you're on your best behaviour, you can watch a PG-13 with Daddy," Damon explains as he leans against the door frame.

Micah turns towards Damon, who hasn't stepped foot inside the door, just like he said he wouldn't. That thought alone is still baffling. After all, this is Damon's house, his rules, and yet, this is all for Micah.

"What am I supposed to do in here?" Micah asks

"Well, Michelangelo. This is where you can experience life as a child, as an adult."

"I get that, but like, why?" He still doesn't understand this world, but he's trying to, at least for today.

"Because our childhoods shape who we become as adults."

"Why is it every time I ask a question, you're giving me some meaning of life response?"

Damon smirks and crosses his arms as he continues to lean against the door. "Because that's got a lot to do with the BDSM world. Not all of it is trauma response or finding a new vice, but it's generally connected to something we can't get from our everyday lives."

"Jesus Christ, would you just step inside the damn door? It's weirding me out." The second Micah gives the order, Damon walks into the room and doesn't stop until he is standing face-to-face with Micah.

"Michelangelo," Damon purrs his name. It makes his body quiver.

"Why do you keep calling me that?"

A tender hand comes up and lifts Micah's chin, so Damon is looking deeply into his eyes.

"It's your name. And what a beautiful name it is." Damon's thumb caresses his chin. "When you're in Little Space, it's what I wish to call you, *if* that's okay with you."

Micah simply nods, his mind clouded from the touch and the mesmerising stare from those green eyes.

"Good." Damon removes his hand and Micah feels like he can breathe again. "There is one more thing." Damon steps towards a wardrobe and slides the door open. Inside, Micah can see an array of board games, children's books, and construction toys, but all of it is forgotten when he sees Damon reach for an article of clothing.

"You're not age-playing or regressing, however, no Little would feel comfortable in tight jeans and a button-up shirt, so…" An oversized T-shirt is handed to him. "When you're a Little, you can wear this. It's soft, loose, and there are also Ninja Turtle pyjama pants to go with it or Jurassic Park pyjama shorts. I'll make sure to have it washed for you to wear each week, though I can always get more."

"So, I just wear this and play in the room?" Suddenly it doesn't sound like such a bad deal.

"Well, there will still be rules. Every child has rules." Damon grins.

"And what's that, hmm?" Micah raises his eyebrows as he sucks in his bottom lip.

"You're to clean up after yourself. Everything in this room is to be returned the way you found it. There is to be no swearing."

"The fu—" Micah cuts himself off when he sees Damon hold a hand up.

Since when does that silence him?

"Daddy's Little does not know such vulgar language."

He bites his tongue, giving a stern nod for Damon to continue.

"You get two movies a day, that is all. If you want video games, that's one movie and one hour of video games. The rest of your time is to be used to stimulate your mind."

"I know another way that's more stimulating," he whispers under his breath. He's sure Damon caught on to what he said but is choosing to ignore it.

"Every Sunday, I want you to write one letter to yourself that has something positive you love about who you are or your body."

"Now I'm doing schoolwork?"

"No. You're creating a positive space for your body and mind. Our childhoods can impact how we tend to be in relationships, in times of stress or change, or when faced with tricky decisions. Your Little is going to help you, over time, expand on those parts of your life."

Micah groans, just like he did when teachers would give out homework.

"There is no touching yourself."

He begins to argue.

"Uh-uh, none. That's for Friday and Saturday only."

A ding goes off in Micah's head when Saturday gets mentioned since he thought that was reserved for spankings only.

"You will eat what I offer and if you eat it all without complaining, I'll be sure to give you a treat."

Damon turns back towards the wardrobe, seemingly on the hunt for something while Micah wonders how people don't see this strict structure as a punishment.

LITTLE ONE

"You'll be in Little Space from nine a.m. until seven p.m. However," Damon turns back to face him and, in his hand, Micah spots a light brown teddy bear. "*If* you ever need to be in Little Space, and it's not a Sunday, just get this teddy and I'll know."

Micah eyes the bear like it's some kind of trick. It's not overly big, just a little smaller than the length of a school ruler. Its fabric looks fluffy, as though he could run his fingers through its fur and it would leave a trail in its place. Micah goes to reach for it, cautiously, and as he accepts the teddy, he instantly notices how soft and squishy it is. The best kind of bear for bedtime cuddles.

"I, ah, I used to have one like this when I was a kid. Called it Bear because I wasn't creative enough to think of anything besides what it actually was." His fingers touch the teddy's ears and trace over the button eyes. "I used to take it with me everywhere, but the older I got, the more my father demanded I got rid of it. Claimed it was childish. Wanted me to grow up and not be dependent on toys."

A memory he had long forgotten suddenly comes flooding back

"I came home to find the head and arms ripped off after my father demanded I not take it to school that day. He said I was naïve to think life could be easier because of a stuffed toy. He forced me to sit in the corner and pray for strength, courage, and forgiveness that I did not have these qualities…I was seven."

"He's yours now, Michelangelo. No one is taking it away. And whenever I see you holding him, I'll be here for whatever you need. When words may be difficult, I'll understand if you have the bear in your arms."

Micah sniffs, not wanting to let his emotions get to him. He's thankful that Damon doesn't touch on the memory, but merely takes it in and moves on.

"Is that it? Or are you going to tell me I have to ask permission to take a piss?" he bites back, trying to bring himself to the present.

"You break any rules and there will be punishment. Corner time. Writing lines or apology letters. You do something to purposely hurt yourself and together, we'll discuss a suitable punishment. If it's big enough, things in this room will be taken away from you." Damon takes a step forward, crowding his personal space. "Lastly, the only name you will call me is Daddy…understood, Michelangelo?" The way Damon says his name is smooth and velvety. Damon leans toward his ear, the slight height difference has the brunet towering over him. "And don't fight it. After the last few days, I've noticed how much your body enjoys calling me *Daddy*."

"Thought you said nothing sexual while I'm being a kid," he fights back, only to avoid the blush he can feel creeping up his chest.

"And I meant it." Damon steps away, giving him more space. "I can be a Daddy by caring for you, and then I can be a Dom Daddy by fulfilling your every desire."

Micah gulps.

Damon moves to walk out of the room. "I'll let you change."

"Why? I'm wearing almost the same thing."

"True. But you're wearing Daddy's clothes, not Little clothes. If you want to immerse into the role, you need to look and feel the part. I'm going to clean up and prepare lunch. Call me if you need anything."

"Yeah, yeah."

Damon stops and turns back toward him with a cocked eyebrow.

"Yes… *Daddy*."

"Good boy." Damon smiles and leaves the room. Meanwhile, Micah is left trying to process the multitude of emotions and questions running through his mind. He decides, like most things in his life, to ignore them. He unbuttons his shirt and pulls on the black cotton T-shirt that ends past his ass. There's a mirror on the wall. He removes the sweatpants that he's wearing and checks himself out. Turning, he lifts the shirt just enough to see his pink-hued ass, some light purple blemishes already appearing in areas.

He opts for the pyjama pants and then looks around the room. "Well, guess it's been a while since I've watched a movie," he says out loud, though as his hands reach out for the light brown bear that is sitting on the wooden table, a part of him wonders if it is the bear he is talking to or himself. Convincing his subconscious that it's all part of the act, he takes the bear over to the beanbag and falls into the pillow of beans as he begins to scroll Disney+.

He's chuckling away at *Toy Story*, a movie he hasn't watched since he was probably three or four. He used to love Buzz, the character's thrill for adventure reflecting a part of himself that he yearned for as a child.

"Knock, knock." He turns to the words, rather than the sound of Damon at the door, who looks relaxed and content, smiling softly at Micah as he sits in the large beanbag with his teddy.

"Lunchtime," Damon announces. "Did you want to eat in here or...?"

"If I leave the room, am I still a Little?"

"Yes. You can be a Little anywhere. This is merely your space, dedicated to you. But if you wanted to go somewhere else in the house, you would still be spending the day as a Little."

He nods and then motions to the wooden table that is set up for what he assumes will be colouring and crafts. He pulls himself from the beanbag and notices Damon still standing at the doorway.

"Seriously?" He huffs. "I motioned towards the table."

"Yes, but you didn't give me verbal permission."

Micah rolls his eyes. "Fine. Come on in, Daddy." He says the name sarcastically, on purpose, just to prove something. Whether it's to himself or Damon, he isn't too sure.

They sit at the table. Micah finds an angle to help with his ass, something he forgot while enjoying the squishiness of the beanbag.

"Would you like a pillow?" Damon asks.

"Defeats the purpose, doesn't it?"

"There is an enjoyable pain and then one of discomfort. The last thing I want is for you to be putting yourself through pain to try to act like you aren't a princess."

"Well, I'm not." Micah takes a bite of the sandwich. There's a small pile of potato chips sitting beside it on a plastic plate, which he's tempted to eat first, but he suspects that is his treat for eating his lunch.

"I never said you are, only to not put yourself through pain so you aren't portraying yourself as one."

"I can handle it. I'm tough." He sits up straight to emphasise his point.

"I know you are." Damon stays calm, not at all offended by Micah's demeanour.

"I can take care of myself."

"You have," Damon offers. "You still do, and you always will. But now, I'm offering to take the lead at times so that you don't have to…so we can take care of each other."

Although Micah wants to know how exactly he's helping to take care of Damon when it seems Damon is doing all the work in this Daddy Little situation they have going on, he decides to let it be and continues to eat in comfortable silence.

It's only when he's finished that he scans the room, taking in all the finer details that he hadn't noticed before. His eyes land on a box in the wardrobe, peeking out from the open door.

"Oh, shit." He instantly cringes.

"Michelangelo, what did I say about language?"

"Oh, come on. One slip-up. I've been swearing since I learnt it was a way to rebel against my parents. What do you want from me?"

"First and only warning. After that, you'll be writing out lines, young man." Damon takes a sip of his glass of water. "What was it you were going to say before your mishap?"

"What I *was* going to ask, was if that's Lego." He points to a box.

Damon doesn't even turn to see what he is pointing at. "Yes, I thought you might like to build something with your time."

"Fu—" He stops himself. "Hell yeah." He wants to laugh at the way Damon is shaking his head at him. "One year, all I wanted for Christmas was the vintage pirate ship," he begins sharing his story. He isn't used to talking about his past so openly, but something about the situation reassures him he can do so without Damon judging or pitying him. "I mean, back then it probably wasn't vintage, but these days that's what it's most likely called. Anyway, I wouldn't shut—*stop* talking about it. I kept telling my friends at school that Santa was going to bring it for me, and I made sure I was on my best behaviour because Santa doesn't bring presents to naughty boys."

He holds his hands out in an 'obviously' kind of way, adding emphasis to his story.

"Anyway." He shoves a few potato chips in his mouth and although he's about to continue with his story, a voice in his head tells him to chew and swallow first.

Weird.

"So, there I am Christmas morning. I open the box that looks exactly like the Lego pirate ship and rip into it."

"And…was it?"

"It was." He smiles, but it fades when he remembers the next part of the story. "Only my father then told me that every gift under the tree was being donated to charity and that the best gift of all was knowing I was worthy of such gifts."

He begins to pick away at the potato chips, signalling that his story is finished, his mind now stuck in the past.

"I'm sorry that's the memory you have. It was wrong of your father to not only take away that illusion of what being good means, that you'll receive gifts from Santa, a tale that creates such an imaginative world for us as children, but to then take away your reward…that's one of the cruellest forms of mind games a parent can play on a child. Especially if they hadn't done anything wrong."

All Micah can do is shrug. Apologies don't mean anything now, especially if they aren't from the people who hurt him. He reaches for his cup of what looks to be apple juice, only to hold the cup midway to his mouth as his eyes catch the words printed on it.

"Really?" He tilts his head to the side.

"What? *You're* my Little One and that cup simply says 'Daddy's Little One.'"

He chugs the whole thing and as he places the cup down, he burps, a sign of satisfaction.

"What do you say, Michelangelo?"

He looks around the room as though he's searching for the answer.

"Ah…thanks?"

"Excuse yourself for being so rude at the table."

"Excuse myself?"

"Yes, you say 'pardon me.'"

"I know what you say but that doesn't mean I'm gonna say it."

"Manners are very important. They help you become more socially attentive."

"Pfft, like I care how people see me."

"Sometimes it's not just about how people see you, Michelangelo, but it's how you see yourself in the eyes of others. How you treat yourself plays into that."

Damon grabs the plates and empty cups, and walks out the door, leaving Micah sitting there feeling as though he's in the Twilight Zone. He mouths the words 'What the fuck' in case Damon is still in earshot.

On the one hand, he can still feel the way Damon stretched him open with his dick as he moaned filth into his ear. On the other hand, Damon has made him feel like his behaviour makes him unworthy, even though he explained how Micah should hold himself to better standards. Micah runs his hands down his face, wondering yet again what it is he is doing here. What do manners and crafting have to do with anything? Why does being called a 'good boy' cause his spine to straighten and his legs to tremble? And how the hell does Damon go from fucking him senseless to acting like a doting Daddy?

He grabs one of the colouring books, almost tearing off the page as he opens it at random, reaching for a green pencil before he begins to shade in the outline.

"This is such a waste of time. I don't know why you're still here," he says out loud, watching to make sure the green stays within the lines. "Sure, the sex is amazing and that spanking…best you've ever had, but still…" He reaches for another shade of green, one that's lighter with a hint of yellow in it. "What? Damon thinks from the two seconds we've had to talk to one another that he knows my childhood, how I was brought up?" He doesn't like how the green is contrasting with the first shade. He swaps it for a light brown and then colours over it. "He thinks this is going to heal me or something? *Please*, it's stupid. That's what it is. I don't need healing. If I wanted that, I would have stayed with my parents and asked for this demon to leave my body," he recites the phrase his parents had once spat at him. "I just need to get laid. I'm free now, so let me be me."

He sits back, looking at his work, opting for a darker brown to go with his already mixed colours. He leans forward in his chair and a twinge in his ass shoots up his back. He loves it.

The monologue dies down and instead, he focuses on the face on the page, the one he has given green eyes, mimicking Damon's. He has shades of brown for the hair and pink for the outline of lips, the lower one clamped between teeth.

Micah marvels at the finished product. He's surprised that not only did he complete it but he's now feeling calmer than he did when he started. The sound of a throat being cleared has him spinning around to the door.

Standing there is Damon, his hair a little dishevelled. *Has he been running his hands through it?* It looks good, the wisp of a curl hanging over his forehead.

"They say colouring is a healthy way to relieve stress." Damon's tone is tender and comforting. "It calms the brain and helps the body to relax. It can improve sleep and fatigue, decrease body aches, heart rate, respiration, even feelings of depression and anxiety."

"You Google now?" It's all he can say. He feels vulnerable, like he needs to guard himself. But Damon doesn't offer any witty or sarcastic comeback.

Micah looks down at his completed picture and takes in Damon's words. These facts that he spouts out of nowhere are clues to help him piece together the puzzle in his mind. He thinks he's beginning to understand why Damon does it, and what he's hoping it will achieve by helping Micah understand this world along with the one he was chasing at the BDSM club.

Standing from the wooden chair, the one that is purposely too small for someone his size and yet was comfortable to sit in while he coloured away, a groan falls from his lips. Not from the chair, but from his ass moving into a new position, causing his muscles to ache and his bruised skin to throb. He reaches for the teddy on the floor beside him. Why, he can't say. But a small part of him knows it's to have the comfort of the soft fabric in his hands.

Feeling somewhat nervous, he walks towards Damon, and as he reaches the entryway, he looks down at his teddy, his hands running up and down the soft fur. It's grounding him. As he realises this, a small part of him finally begins to understand that maybe this process could open a part of him that he never knew existed.

He knows they are both sorry for their behaviour regarding manners. It's only been three days, but he has begun to understand how to read Damon's body language. The way he stands at the door on edge, his body tense as though he has been working himself up into an overthought panic. Only to deflate with relief once Micah offers a sarcastic remark to break the ice. Perhaps Damon is concerned that he's pushing too hard too fast. Either way, Micah knows what he wants to do, and so he does what he was told and asks for it.

"Can Daddy please sit with me and watch a movie?" With bated breath, Micah's body relaxes the second he feels that familiar finger under his chin, raising his head so their eyes meet once again.

"I'd love to sit with my Little One. Thank you for asking me, Michelangelo."

Micah takes Damon's hand and leads them to the large round beanbag. He stands as Damon sits in it first, leaving a space beside him for Micah to sink into, their bodies moulding together as they sag deeper, a soft barrier forming around them.

"What does my Little One wish to watch?"

"Tarzan, the live-action."

"Michelangelo." Damon's voice is stern.

"Okay, okay. Cartoon version. Thought I'd at least try." He nuzzles his head onto Damon's shoulder, taking comfort in the closeness and warmth. Micah wraps both of his arms around his teddy bear as kisses are laid on his forehead. Then there is a whisper against his skin, "Maybe one day, as a special treat, we can watch the live-action one together."

As Damon presses play, his arm pulls Micah in closer, wrapping around him. Micah considers that Damon's 'one day' might be more plausible than he thought when he first woke up this morning.

Chapter 7
Deal

When Micah gets home on Sunday night, he feels refreshed and settled. The quietness inside his head allows him to stop and breathe for a change. It's unfamiliar territory to what he's used to—a racing mind and fidgeting energy.

On Monday, his skin has the purple and yellow hues of an ass well-spanked. The best part is that he completely forgets about it until he sits down and feels the tender muscle that still aches.

By Tuesday, his mind is made up. There is no point denying that he wants to agree to the contract, permanently. It is all he can think about. The opportunity to do it again, being Damon's only focus, basking in all the pleasures and pain.

> Micah
> I'm in. All of it. No more trial runs.

As though Damon has been watching his phone religiously, Micah receives a reply instantly.

> Damon
> Are you sure? You were comfortable with everything?

> Still weird, but yeah. I think I'm starting to get the whole Little Space.

> Okay. I'll get the new contracts organised.

Micah is about to jump in the shower when another message comes through.

Damon
> I'm glad you said yes, Micah. I don't think I could have let you go so easily had you said no.

He doesn't reply, but he does jerk off in the shower to visuals of Damon's hand, his lips, and the way Damon's mouth formed the perfect O when he came inside of him.

His ass cheeks are itchy all day Wednesday. He finds himself hiding in parts of the bookstore no one can see so he can give himself a good scratch, positive he will break the skin if he isn't careful.

He messages Damon on his lunch break, asking if it's normal since he hasn't had such a reaction in the past.

Damon
> Very normal. Unlike your other spankings, mine got deep into your tissue, not just a pounding of your flesh. Now your body is healing by sending cells to the area, which causes inflammation and itchiness. Put some cream on it. I would if I were there but the best I can do is offer my help rather than give it.

Seconds later, another text message comes through with a click-and-collect notice for some soothing cream Damon has purchased, with instructions to retrieve it on his way home.

Micah

> You didn't have to pay for it. All I needed was the name.

> Your role is not to question my monetary decisions. A Daddy's job is to provide for his Little One's health and happiness. If you need it, I'll supply it. Simple as that.

> We're not playing. I'm working.

> And I'm not asking. I'm telling. Because of how we played, you need treatment. Now be a good boy and do as you're told.

Micah sighs and pockets his phone. Suddenly, something comes over him, something he will claim he did out of obligation rather than the simple desire to do so. He removes his phone and opens his contacts. Under Damon's name, he clicks edit and changes the name to Daddy.

The cream helps with the itchiness, which is why he can't understand what has him tossing and turning later in bed. Wide awake, he begins to scroll through his phone. Random videos on his timeline bore him, but not enough to close his eyes and sleep. The search through his favourite porn sites isn't of interest to him, so he decides to look over his messages from Dam—*Daddy*. Referring to Damon as Daddy is going to take time, but seeing the title at the top of their text thread is another step closer.

When he gets to their most recent messages, he quickly realises why his mind won't settle. He hasn't said thank you for the cream. Once the realisation hits, he's surprised at the sheer disappointment he feels at himself for not expressing his appreciation for Damon's kind gesture…to *Daddy's* kind gesture. And when that notion hits him, he realises how deep into this role he's gotten himself, and so quickly.

Regardless of the hour, he sends a message.

Micah

Thank you…for the cream. It helped.

The second he presses send, his eyes begin to droop and sleep finally takes over.

The next night has him feeling a little out of routine. Generally, he'd be getting ready to hit the club, but now that his deal with Damon has certain rules, that isn't an option. So, he goes directly to the source.

LITTLE ONE

Micah
> Feels weird not going to the club. Could this week go any bloody slower?

Daddy
> I must admit, the club is not as entertaining as it was when I knew you were coming.

Micah
> Wait! You're there?

Daddy
> Of course.

Micah
> The fuck! Thought you said we're exclusive or whatever.

Daddy
> We are. I'm merely sitting here, watching, thinking of all the things I'm going to do to you tomorrow night while I take notes on ways to flip this business once I own it.

He bites his bottom lip.

Why does Damon being at the club make him feel unsettled?
Why does he care so much?
Why does he feel as though trust has been broken?

Micah's lack of reply must trigger something from Damon because suddenly, his phone rings in his hand.

Daddy's name appears on the screen, and he decides to let it go to voicemail, not ready to listen to any excuse. Once the ringing stops, he quickly sends off a text.

Micah
> Going to bed. Don't call. I have an early start.

★★★

Damon paces his living area with a tumbler of whiskey in each hand, hoping, *praying* that the plans for this evening are still on. When the elevator doors open, he stops. Out walks a cautious Micah. Damon hands him a glass and Micah downs the drink in one gulp, eyes diverting to the paperwork sitting on the coffee table.

"That desperate to get me to sign, huh?"

"No, Micah," he speaks from the heart. "I'd never pressure you into anything you weren't a hundred per cent certain of." Damon takes a sip of his whiskey as he walks towards the couch, sitting as he motions with his head for Micah to follow.

"I want to talk about last night," Damon begins.

"Not what I came here for," Micah bites back.

"*Micah.*"

"No. I get it. You gotta do what you gotta do for your business. It is what it is."

"You're upset. I need to know why."

Micah scoffs, "Yeah, me too." The words are a whisper but not low enough for Damon to miss it.

"Do you not trust me?"

"I don't trust anyone. Never had a reason to. My life has always been filled with the belief of some higher power that turned everyone I loved against me all because of who I chose to share my bed with."

"I wasn't accusing you, Micah. I just want to understand what I did to disappoint you."

"Did you get what you needed?" Micah's gripping the glass so tight his knuckles are white.

"I sat in a chair all night looking at my phone, hoping it would ring."

Damon waits until hazel eyes look into his green ones. Only then does he continue, knowing he has Micah's full attention.

"I know we just met. I know you have no reason to believe anything I say, but if you can trust me with your body, please, try to trust me on this. Know that I *did not* and *will not* break the rules of our contract."

Damon's expecting questions, perhaps even a demand for proof that he didn't break their contract of being exclusive. What he isn't expecting is Micah to reach for the pen and sign the new contract. The one that is the same as the first, except it's no longer on a trial basis.

When Micah drops the pen, he looks surprised.

"What? Find someone new last night? Don't want to sign it anymore?" The words are full of venom.

Damon stands from the couch and walks to his drink cart, filling his glass with another dash of whiskey.

"My last relationship, not a contract, but an actual relationship, ended when my partner left me for someone younger. Someone who dabbled in this lifestyle." He pauses. "I can separate myself from this world when need be, but you need to understand that *I am* this world."

"Why are you telling me this?" Damon can hear the confusion in Micah's voice.

"For two reasons." Damon still has his back to Micah. "You lived in my world for three days, not even a week, and yet you signed your body over to me without a moment to think about what you're agreeing to."

"You make it sound like I've joined a cult."

Damon huffs, a chuckle of sorts. He can see Micah's face in the glass reflection, but he still refuses to look his way. "This isn't a joke for me. This is serious. This is my life. I've had many in the past who think this is what they want but it's not. They decide to leave after I've given so much of myself to them because that's how it works. You give yourself over to me and I in turn do the same."

He finally turns to face Micah. "I'd never force you to stay if you didn't want to. I'd never force you to be locked into the contract, but I can't let you sign it without really understanding what you're agreeing to. It requires a lot, especially for a Dominant, to change their ways to suit each Submissive."

Micah's hands rub together as though to warm them up. "I'm agreeing to having control, while essentially having all my control taken away. I'm agreeing to let you fuck me, spank me, and put me in time out if you believe it's right."

Damon holds his head high with pride and admiration at Micah's answer.

"Control for me isn't to feel powerful, it's to feel balanced. My control over you is so I know you're safe. So you don't get hurt. So you're healthy and taken care of." Damon takes a step forward. "I want to control your pleasure because every one of your orgasms is now for me. Given *to* me, *by* me."

Micah's cheeks flush.

"The second reason I'm telling you this is because, when I realised there was a chance that you were not going to show up tonight, or that you had decided not to continue with our contract…well, that scared the shit out of me." Damon looks down at his drink but doesn't take a sip. "Nothing has scared me like that since I experienced my first Dom Drop."

Damon moves on, not wanting to focus on that negative experience.

"Last weekend was the most exhilarating connection I have felt in a very, *very* long time, Micah."

"We both got over our dry spell. Good for us."

"No, Micah. I'm not just talking about the sex." Damon steps closer and finally sits back down. "That was, *fuck*, that was incredible. But being able to open your world, watching you explore Little Space, the beautiful marks I got to leave on your ass. Those sensations are why I stepped into the BDSM world, and I was beginning to think that I'd never feel them again. Not to that extent. Not with someone who truly wants to let go and give themselves to me."

Micah looks down at his empty glass and Damon can't stand to see the hesitancy in those gorgeous hazel eyes. With a tender touch, he reaches out and gently places his fingers under Micah's chin. The gentle pressure is a silent request for Micah to raise his head and look directly at him.

"You're what I've been looking for, Micah. What I've been missing. I have everything in this world but it's futile if I can't express the deepest, truest part of myself." Damon moves his hand from Micah's chin and cups the side of his face. "So please, trust me when I say *nothing* happened at the club and *nothing* ever will." His thumb caresses a soft cheek. "And if it truly troubles you, I'll stop attending, unless you are by my side."

"Look, I'm not going to ask you to stop going. I get it, it's business. It's just," hazel eyes look around the room before they land back on Damon, "it fucking caught me off guard, okay? This," Micah's hands gesture between them, "this is a whole new ball game for me, and I don't want to screw it up because nothing good ever happens to me. Everything I've always wanted has been taken away from me…it's why I never let anyone in. It's easier."

"Is that why you got angry? Because you let me in?"

There is a sigh of defeat. "I don't know how it happened, and so fast but, *fuck*. What you did, what you gave me and opened my body to…I released the lock on the doors, gave you the key, and allowed you to roam around like you owned the place. And now, *now* I can't stop thinking about it, thinking about you, thinking about wanting more."

"That's why you signed the contract."

"I signed so fucking fast because I didn't want anyone else bending over your lap or being fucked by what's mine."

The word ignites a possessive spark within Damon. His lips crash onto pillowy soft ones the second Micah finishes his sentence.

"Say it again," Damon demands in a deep growl.

"You're *mine*...and now *I'm yours*," Micah pants against his lips.

Hearing that Micah is his sets Damon off. Their kissing continues and it's fierce and messy. Hands grope anywhere in reach, while tongues and teeth mesh together.

Their glasses tumble to the floor. Micah goes to stop, but Damon's hand grips the back of Micah's head, keeping him in place.

"Fucking leave it. I'll buy a new rug if I must," he orders. The desire within him overshadows the damage to his three-thousand-dollar rug. Their hands shed each other's clothing and somehow, without breaking apart, they succeed. He considers fucking Micah right there on the couch until something else comes to mind. Damon wraps his arms around Micah's waist, hoisting him up. Micah's toned legs hook around Damon's hips, their tongues still tasting the liquor in each other's mouths as Damon begins to walk them to the bedroom.

Once naked, skin touching skin, their body heat is enough to keep away the chill of the night air. Damon sits them on the curved arched chair near the balcony window, the one he saw Micah study the first time he stepped foot in the room.

"You going to role-play being my therapist and fuck me in this chair?" Micah jokes, the brat within making a small appearance.

Oh, how quickly he'll have that brat tamed tonight. "No, Micah, I'm going to fuck you by the window so I can imagine all of the city watching me claim you in my tantra sex chair."

"Tantra sex—"

"You heard me. Designed to vastly enhance sex and allow for a more comfortable and easier way to experience the Kama Sutra." Damon speaks as though it should be obvious, but with the twitch of Micah's cock and the lick of his lips, Damon knows he's about to open his Submissive's world to a whole new level of pleasure.

★★★

Micah lies against the leather arch, giving Damon a chance to make his way toward the nightstand. Micah watches Damon's muscles move as he walks, the older man's back ripples and his thighs clench. Micah's breath hitches the second Damon turns back around, his eyes landing on Damon's glorious dick, full mast, bobbing against his stomach as he walks back toward him. The slight curve to the right makes it naturally stand at the perfect angle to hit his prostate when Damon's deep inside of him.

Before Micah has time to swallow the drool that's pooling in his mouth, Damon stands before him, a leg on either side of the chair, while Micah's mouth sits level with a thick, uncut nine-inch cock.

"Does my good boy want a taste?" Fingers run through Micah's hair, and the tip of Daddy's dick drags against his lips.

"*Please*, Daddy. Wanna taste you." Micah isn't even aware that the title slips from his mouth.

"Daddy can't say no to you, especially with manners like that. Open wide, baby."

Micah's mouth falls open and his eyes close as he waits for Daddy to use his mouth like a warm cocksock. As much as he wants to see the ecstasy on Daddy's face as he swallows him down, his mind is too focused on relishing in the sensation of having Daddy's cock leaving more bruises to remember him by.

"Look at you, relaxing your throat so you can take me deeper." Daddy yanks on his hair, forcing his head to tilt back so he can slide further down his throat. Tears spring from the corner of Micah's eyes as his mouth stretches, fighting the urge to gag.

He can taste the saltiness of precum on his tongue, the flavour has Micah whimpering for more.

"Uh-uh-uh. I know you want to, but this load, I want to put elsewhere." Daddy slides himself out of his mouth and with it, Micah takes a large, gulping breath.

"Colour?" Damon checks in.

"Green." Micah's voice is hoarse. He wishes the bruises forming on his throat were ones he could see, much like the ones left on his ass. Daddy sits on the shorter side of the tantra chair, the arch lower than the one currently supporting Micah's back.

"Turn around for Daddy. Show me that glorious ass."

Micah stands on shaky legs, turns and then lays down on the smooth leather, his legs on either side of the seat, leaning forward so his chest presses against the arch. The dip in the chair creates the perfect bow in his back, his ass presented to Daddy.

"*Fuck*, need it." Micah pushes back, the week since their last time together feels like a lifetime.

"*Shhh*, Daddy's got you." Micah melts at the affirmation, and he knows in his heart that Damon does.

Micah is bewildered by the way his body's desire is only heightened each time the title of Daddy is used between them.

As fingers open him, though it's more for pleasure than a necessity since Micah prepared himself before arriving, a part of him wishes his parents could see him now. See the way his body is letting go and accepting the pleasures of another man. See the way he is giving up control, sinning like his mother accused him of. Behaving like the pillow biter he knew he was, relishing being the cum slut his father was disgusted to learn he was.

"You ready, baby?"

Micah's body trembles at the pet name.

"Give it to me, Daddy." Micah turns to look behind himself, seeing Damon sit up, his large hands on either side of Micah's hips as Daddy's red, throbbing cock lines up with his ass. The position has his body at the perfect angle to feel Daddy's length slide inside him. He swears he can feel him in his stomach. He's so full and yet Daddy is only halfway in.

"All week, I couldn't stop thinking about this ass. Thinking about filling it. Tasting it. Owning it."

"According to those papers. *Ungh*. You own more than just this ass. *OH, FUCK.*"

Damon bottoms out and Micah can barely move.

"Take it for me, I know you can," Daddy purrs into his ear.

Micah's hands grip the leather as he takes each thrust, but it's not enough. The animalistic urges inside of him that lay dormant are now awake and hungry. Whatever strength Micah has left, he uses it to balance on his feet, giving him enough leverage to bounce on Daddy's dick.

"Oh, *fuck*, Micah."

"You like that, Daddy?" Micah's attempt at taking control doesn't last long. A hand is suddenly grasping Micah's throat while another grips his hip. There is enough pressure on each area for Micah's body to instinctively know it needs to follow the command of those hands. With nine inches still deep inside of him, he is repositioned so he's sitting on Daddy's lap. The large hand around Micah's throat squeezes just enough so he tilts his head back and rests it against Daddy's shoulder.

"Fuckin' love it. I told you, baby. Your body wants to submit. It craves my control," Daddy whispers in his ear. Micah's body breaks out in goosebumps. "I'm going to breed this ass, plug it, and then breed it again, and again *and again*. Keeping my loads deep inside of you until the pressure becomes too much."

Micah's eyes roll to the back of his head. The pulsing tension around his throat restricts his breathing, only for it to loosen just in time to gasp in lungfuls of air. Daddy's cock is pounding his prostate, Micah's own dick spurting precum, aching to be touched.

"Do it, Daddy. I want it. I want it so fuckin' bad."

The hand around his hip moves away and the second Daddy grips his dick, there is no hope.

"Fuck, *Daddy*." Micah comes so hard a string of cum lands on his chin. The thrusting never stops, adding to his pleasure as hot shots of cum paint his chest and dribble down Daddy's hand.

"*That's my boy*," Daddy purrs.

Micah slumps forward. The grip on his tender dick loosens. The same hand that brought him to his end is placed in front of his face. Without any instructions, Micah laps up his cum that's dripping from his Daddy's hand, moaning in contentment with how sweet he tastes.

"Save some for me, baby."

Cock drunk. Cum drunk. Neither is enough to distract Micah as Daddy lifts him from his throne. Micah's ass clenches, hoping to grip the throbbing dick sliding out of him. Preparing to beg if he has to, Micah stops when he looks over his shoulder to see the remnants of cum on Daddy's hand, being used to lather Daddy's cock, mixing it with the beads of precum that are leaking out of him.

Micah bites his lip in anticipation as two strong hands grip his ass cheeks and spread them. He feels exposed in the best of ways. Daddy stares at him, almost hypnotised by his gaping hole, stretched and winking at him for more. Micah turns back around, wanting to be surprised.

The moment Daddy thrusts back inside of him, the wind gets knocked from Micah's lungs. The sensation of his own cum being pushed inside of him is pornographic.

He loves it.

"Look at that hole. So pink and used. It's the perfect fit for my cock." Daddy's thrusts are painstakingly slow.

At this stage, Micah's body has slipped into the 'ragdoll' phase, allowing Daddy to use him for his pleasure. But when Daddy pulls all the way out and stands up, Micah instantly feels the loss. His body is cold, and his hole is empty.

Hands are immediately manhandling him, lifting Micah from the tantra chair and placing him down on the mattress that feels ten times softer than it did last week.

"Hold your legs for me, baby." Micah obeys, though he isn't sure how long he can, his arms weak and body tired.

Daddy's tip is back at his rim and like the needy bottom he is, whimpers begin to fall from Micah's lips, a plea to be filled.

"You're all mine, Micah. Never wanted anyone else as much as I want you." Micah gasps when Daddy bottoms out and shoots his load deep within him. He feels it, every single moment. The clench of his rim, the heat of Daddy's cum, the pressure from such a large load fills him from the inside, threatening to spill out of him.

As quickly as it happens, Daddy pulls out, but the plug that Micah was promised is pushed inside, holding in every drop as his rim closes around the t-bar plug. Micah moans as the bulb gives him the fullness he aches for whenever Daddy isn't inside of him.

Daddy lays on the mattress beside him as they both pant on their backs, and Micah has no desire to get dressed and run.

"Relax," Micah begins, "I know I gotta stay for the aftercare." He offers a cheeky smirk, but the sex they just had was more than anything he's endured since he became sexually active. Even if he wanted to leave, his body won't allow it.

Micah turns his head to the side, watching as Damon sits up slightly, his elbow holding up his body weight as he rests his head in the palm of his hand.

"You okay?"

Micah groans. "Do I look like that was something I didn't enjoy?"

"That wasn't the question, Micah. What just happened was not only intense, but it had a few power moves that we hadn't discussed."

"If I wasn't into it, I would have told you to fuck off. Simple as that." He closes his eyes because he's too tired to hold them open. Damon's fingertips begin to trail up and down the length of his arm.

"Thank you," Damon eventually says in the quiet of the room.

Micah opens one eye to peek at the older man. "For what? Letting you drop a load in me?"

Damon chuckles. After the solemn mood that took hold from the moment he arrived, it's soothing to hear the sound come from the man beside him.

"Well, that too, but no. I meant thank you for calling me Daddy. I know you had some trepidation with the name."

Micah squirms, making the plug move, and he's instantly reminded of the fantastic pleasure he just endured.

"I guess I kinda get it now, the title…" He always knew a name had power. Unfortunately, he's only ever experienced it in a negative way, like when his father spat derogatory slang at him.

"Each time I said it, I watched you become someone else. This confidence and pride swelled within you." Micah opens his eyes and looks at Damon who is lapping up every word he says. "After last week, I guess I *believe* in the name or whatever." He turns away, eyes closing so he can speak to the darkness. "Like you said, you're guiding me through this experience. You buy me cream and leave me Advil. You own that role, and you own me, so…" he takes a deep breath before facing Damon once again, "guess that makes you my Daddy."

A blinding smile spreads over Damon's face. Damon's hand finds its way to Micah's cheek, holding him in place as he leans forward and plants a tender kiss that's so faint, Micah wonders if he's dreaming.

"Stay," Damon whispers against his lips. "And I promise to make good on my other promise…" Micah cocks an eyebrow. "To fuck you again and again until the pressure of my cum inside of you is so intense that I'll have to clean it out with my tongue."

Holy shit.
No way could he say no to that.

Chapter 8
Spank-a-thon

RACHEL O'ROURKE

It's noon before Micah wakes. His muscles are aching slightly, and his ass burns from being used and abused over and over throughout the night. It's a phenomenal feeling. Daddy did keep his promise, fucking him a further four times until he couldn't take it anymore, and the second the plug was removed, a volcanic eruption of cum squirted straight into his Daddy's mouth.

Once he finds the energy to open his eyes, his mind waking before his body is ready, Micah smiles at the familiar view, the warm sun beaming through the balcony windows and a note beside him on the bedside table.

Good morning, Micah.
I've left a gift out for you to wear. I figured with today's agenda, it might make things much easier and enjoyable for both of us.
Damon.

Curious, he sits up, with a throb here and a twinge there, and walks into the bathroom. He can't help but shake his head at the clothing left for him, smirking at the outfit Damon had in mind.

He showers, ignoring how his body responds to the smell of Damon's body wash, and then gets dressed with no argument about playing along with Damon's plan.

With an eyebrow cocked, he walks into the kitchen, wearing the royal blue jockstrap and a very loose-fitted button-up shirt, which he can only assume belongs to Damon. The hem of the shirt covers his ass, but it wouldn't take much for him to bend over and bare himself to Daddy's magical hands.

"*Mmm*, now aren't you a sight for sore eyes."

"Pretty sure this outfit is more for you than it is for me." Micah sits on the stool, loving the throb of his stretched and tender rim, though he can't deny that he feels confident in a sexy kind of way. Something he's never felt before. Hell, he's never worn anything besides boxer briefs or sometimes just going commando for convenience.

"Oh, it's *all* for me, but by the time I'm finished, you're not going to want any fabric touching that delicious bo—"

"Be careful of your next choice of words there, Stone." Micah steals a piece of fruit from the plate Damon prepared, smirking at the fun, easy banter between them.

Breakfast is eaten, conversation is exchanged, and Micah can't believe how willingly he opens up to Damon when prompted. Discussions about his childhood, as psychologically damaging as it was, flow freely from his lips. Damon shares stories about his upbringing, which led him to this lifestyle. It doesn't go unnoticed that Damon avoids mentioning partners from the past, something he had no issues doing before signing the contract.

With empty plates before them and truths being shared, Micah broaches the subject of last night.

"Can I ask you something?"

"You don't have to *ask* to ask me something, Micah." Damon takes a sip of his coffee. "But from the tone of your voice, you're unsure how I'll react to your question."

He really can read people.

"Ask away, I won't bite…unless you want me to," he says with a wink.

"Last night you mentioned Dom Drop…what exactly is that?"

At times, he forgets that Damon is ten years older than him, only to be reminded when he holds himself a certain way, like now. The question has Damon crossing his legs, leaning back into the dining chair with his fingers linked, resting on top of his knee.

"Based on your question, I'm assuming you don't know what a Sub Drop is either."

Micah answers with a shake of his head.

"It's one of the reasons why I'm so adamant on aftercare. A drop, whether it be Submissive or Dominant, is basically the same, but they happen for different reasons. It occurs from an emotional or physical low, and it can appear within hours or perhaps a few days of an emotional and endorphin high. That feeling after I spanked you last week, that cloud you were floating on…"

Micah nods to show he remembers it well.

"Had you been in that headspace, and I forced you to stand, get dressed and go back home, there is no doubt in my mind you would have dropped. Pulling the mind out of an endorphin high abruptly can cause a crash, a depression of sorts. Everyone experiences it differently; some can feel rejected or used. For some, their body goes into shock. A scene leaves both parties feeling vulnerable and that's why we must be brought back slowly after playing to avoid the drop in our mood."

"So, you had a Dom Drop because you stopped playing too quickly?"

"More or less. That is the element that is the same between the two, the part that differentiates them is the exhaustion that comes from being a Dominant," Damon explains. "During a scene, we experience a wide spectrum of positive emotions, but if we play too hard for too long, and step back into reality too quickly, we drop. If we allow society's influence to get to our heads, and make us question the type of person we are based on what we enjoy doing, it can mess with our psyche, creating doubt, which is never safe for a Dom or a Sub." Damon stops, like he's making sure the seriousness of the conversation has time to sink in.

"When we play, Micah, I'm not only taking care of myself but of you also. You trust me to take care of your body and mind, to understand what you need. You can imagine the kind of energy that can drain from a person." Damon pauses. "I didn't know all this when I first started, and not knowing put me at more of a risk. I was essentially feeding it, causing myself to drop more frequently and for longer periods because I was overexerting my mind and body. My mentor found me the night I made my first and *only* mistake. I put my Sub at risk because I wasn't focused and that is why *I* need aftercare as much as any of my Subs do. To make sure nothing like that ever happens again."

Micah doesn't need to know what danger Damon is referring to. It was in the past and had he, at any time, not felt safe while they had been playing, he would have up and left in a heartbeat.

"I'll be sure to look for the signs. That way I can get you out before you go to the bad place." The smile Damon offers him is proof he said the right thing, that he's learning, understanding, and for that, he feels proud.

"Are you ready for your first spanking then, or do you have some more questions?" Damon asks outright.

Micah swallows. A thrilling excitement runs through him.

"Here?" It's all he can respond with. He watches as Damon pushes his chair back and pats his lap. Damon's grey cashmere sweatpants look soft, complimenting his black, loosely fitted T-shirt.

He stands, takes a step forward and leans over Damon's lap. As Micah bends, his shirt rises, putting his perfectly rounded cheeks, curved by the jockstrap, proudly on display for Daddy to do as he wants.

"How would you like it, Micah?" The tone indicates that Damon is gone, and Daddy has taken his place. A comforting hand begins to rub over Micah's cheeks, warming the skin, or teasing him, perhaps both.

"The second one." His mind recalls the way Daddy's hand cupped his ass like he was holding something delicate, holding *him* delicately.

"Colours?"

"Green. Yellow. Red." He waits, only to realise that so is Daddy. "I'm green."

"Close your eyes, just let yourself feel."

Micah follows Daddy's orders. He has no reason to fight it. *This* is what he wants, what he signed up for.

The smacks come one by one. The first is a shock, the sound louder than the pressure, but then the noise is almost like a distant hum and Micah does as Daddy tells him to and lets. Himself. Feel.

His ass takes each spank until it can't. Until the warmth spreads across his cheeks and the break between each smack is enough for his brain to register what's happening, a moment for his tissue to feel tender before another blow makes an impact.

It stops. Micah isn't sure how long he lies over Daddy's lap before the spanking eases up, or how many spanks he took, but his body is too tranquil to move.

"Take it easy, don't rush to get up. Remember what we just spoke about."

Legs like jelly, Micah stands, a calmness washing over him like waves hitting the sandy shore. He doesn't dare to move, *or could it be because Daddy hasn't told him to?* A cold glass is pressed against his lips. He drinks. The refreshing water helps his mind refocus.

"When you're ready, come to me and I'll spank you again. *This* is for you. I want to hear when you want it and how; because you're in control."

Micah exhales and then, without thinking, walks towards the couch where he lays on his stomach and takes in the city view. He feels Damon's presence, hovering. It reminds him of a puppy waiting to be told he can jump on the bed.

"Why do I feel like I'm high?"

The dip in the couch calms him further. "Spanking stimulates your skin's nerve receptors. It triggers a release of endorphins and dopamine."

"You're like a walking encyclopedia, aren't you?" he mumbles against the couch cushion.

The huff Damon lets out is endearing. "It's my duty to understand why and what our bodies do if I'm going to treat it a certain way."

"Funny how my body never responded this way after my dad gave me a belting." The words slip, but the gentle hand on his back eases the panic that would have originally surfaced had he shared that information with someone random. Someone whom he hasn't entrusted his body with.

"Pain for pleasure and pain for punishment are very different. And although people in the BDSM community partake in inflicting pain due to punishment, those people generally need it for other situations."

"You saying I like being hit?"

"The opposite, actually. When you were being beaten, you had no power. Now, the power is all yours."

Micah turns slightly so his eyes can lock with Damon's as he continues.

"Your body can relax knowing you don't have to think or take responsibility for what's about to happen because *you know* what's going to happen. You know how it will end so your mind and body can switch off and for once, soak in those endorphins."

Damon's hand reaches out and runs his fingers through Micah's hair, the sensation soothing beyond belief.

"You don't want to be spanked because you have trauma, Micah. You want to be spanked because you spend your day hyper-focused on your surroundings. On what you say and do in your work and social environment. You want to be spanked because, for those few moments, you have silence. You can break down your walls and just be."

After half an hour, Micah asks Daddy for another spanking. This time, Micah places his hands on the glass window that overlooks the city and soaks in each smack.

Once it's over, he turns around and tells Daddy he's ready to see the library upstairs. He's taking charge, just like he was told he could do.

Each step pulls at his skin, and it doesn't go unnoticed that although Damon is directing him to *his* home library, he decides to stand behind Micah as he ascends the stairs.

Perhaps he should buy a few pairs of jockstraps to surprise Daddy with.

The library is stunning. Deep, mahogany shelves cover all four walls, including the back of the door Micah walked through. There is a skylight that shines onto a high-back pincushion chair with a small table beside it.

"As you can see, there is room to grow my collection." Micah turns to see a bashful-looking Damon.

"Relax, I'm not going to judge you on your empty shelves." He browses what's on display, categorised by genre. There are books that Damon no doubt read while learning his craft. Non-fiction novels from people with mental health issues. An array of LGBTQIA+ fiction stories and a few true crimes and thrillers.

"Pick what you like. You can read it here or come back down. I'll be around when you're ready." Damon walks out the door. As Micah's left to peruse, not an ounce of him feels self-conscious in his attire.

He runs his fingers along the spine of the LGBTQIA+ books, randomly selecting one to flip through while he leans against the wall. He barely gets through the first chapter before he wanders off with the book in hand to find his Daddy for another spanking.

Damon looks at him in surprise. "Are we on a half-hour schedule?"

Playfully biting his lip, Micah says nothing as he presents himself in a downward dog position on the leather couch for this round.

"Any requests?" Daddy asks as he rubs Micah's already tender cheeks.

"Do as you please, Daddy." Micah's found that the title for Damon is easiest to say when they are in a scene and playing, but he's not ready to use it openly during a discussion or a meal.

For his third spanking today, Micah feels cared for and nurtured from start to finish, including the downtime in-between; true Daddy-like behaviour.

The slaps are firmer this time, and he finds his face getting pushed against the leather with each blow. Eventually, he finds himself using the book as a place to rest his head until Daddy decides to stop, rubbing his skin tenderly to ease the sting.

"How do you feel?"

"It's more intense at the start now that I've gone a few rounds, but then it's like the pain vanishes until it decides to come back ten times stronger." Micah kneels on the couch, his ass not ready to fully seat itself.

"The human body is designed to withstand certain levels of pain. It registers what's happening, responds to it, and eventually, if it continues to happen, the brain turns the pain receptors off so that the body can no longer feel it."

"That's what happened," Micah admits. "It was like I could feel your hand but not what it did until my ass became sore 'n each blow was more tender and less pleasurable."

"Eventually though, even that becomes too much for the brain to mask," Damon explains. "I noticed the second your body began to register the impact because you began to flinch." Damon walks towards the kitchen and Micah follows him with his eyes, trying to understand why the man looks sexy as hell when all he's doing is retrieving a glass of water.

"Here." Damon passes him the glass. "Drink. You need to stay hydrated. I'll make us something to eat."

Somehow, a thirty-minute interval between spanks became silently agreed upon and Micah isn't complaining. His mind is calm. He finds himself smiling more and is genuinely interested in talking to Damon about anything and everything in between.

However, it's around the ninth spanking when Micah understands why Damon has provided him with his outfit for the day. He hisses the second his cheeks brush against fabric or sits on the leather. His bare ass is a relief.

Damon's apartment is warm, the central heating and the fireplace doing their job, yet Micah's body begins to feel cold. Perhaps it's due to only wearing a jockstrap and button-up. He stands after he thanks his Daddy for another spanking, catching the glint in his vibrant green eyes and the way his Daddy's face looks as calm and relaxed as he feels. But then Micah's body begins to tremble, increasing to an intensity he has no control over.

"Micah? Micah, are you okay?" Damon places his hands on Micah's biceps. Micah knows the touch is to try and settle him but it doesn't seem to make a difference. He tries to tense his muscles, to distract his mind and ease the quivering of his body. It doesn't work. His teeth begin to chatter.

"Shit. Your body's going into shock. Come here."

Micah doesn't speak, he simply allows himself to be manhandled onto the couch where he's placed to sit carefully against Damon's side. Damon drapes his arm over his shoulder so he can nuzzle into Damon's chest. A throw blanket covers his legs, which are manoeuvred to rest on top of Damon's lap, but Damon makes a point not to cover his upper body.

"Da-Damon, what i-is hap-hap-happening?" Micah finally gets out.

"You're overstimulated," Damon calmly explains as his hand rubs up and down Micah's arm. "Your body is trying to naturally cool itself down because of the excessive heat of your cheeks. Because the rest of your body isn't producing the same heat on your skin, you're going into shock."

Micah can already feel himself warming, his teeth stop chattering but his body still trembles.

"I'm sorry," Damon confesses.

"What," he steadies his breathing, "for?"

"I should have known better. It's been a few years since I've partaken in multiple spankings throughout the day." Damon pulls him in closer. "I was planning to offer the soothing gel to you at the end, but I should have been applying it after every scene."

"Damon," Micah's voice is soft, but he feels like himself again.

"Aftercare. The number one rule. I should have enforced it each time we were done. And after the conversation we had this morning."

"Damon," he speaks a little louder, his body no longer trembling.

"Did you drink enough water? I'm sure you did. I made sure to get you a glass after each round. But then did you drink it? What about—"

"Daddy!" He doesn't scream the word, but he makes sure to say it with enough authority that it grabs Damon's attention.

"You did *nothing* wrong." Their eyes lock. Micah makes sure he doesn't blink until the fear seeps out of Damon's eyes. "You said it yourself. My body is just overstimulated. Even though *I* could take it, it's not used to this much attention. This kind of activity so frequently."

Although they've never done it outside of sex, Micah has the urge to lean in and kiss the concern away from the man before him, so he does.

It's tender. Delicate. Pillowy-soft lips land on juicy sweet ones.

Damon's hand reaches up and lands on the side of Micah's face, holding him against his lips. Micah melts into his touch. Damon's taste centres Micah after the ordeal his body has been through.

Eventually, reluctantly, they separate, if only to get oxygen back into their lungs. Damon keeps his hand on Micah's face, his soft padded thumb rubs against his cheekbone and Micah can't help but rest his forehead against Damon's.

"You called me Daddy outside of a scene."

"Needed to get your attention." Micah keeps his eyes down.

"Hmm, well it worked."

Micah exhales and then slowly looks back up into forest-green eyes. "Besides, that's who you are…my Daddy." He doesn't miss the slight hitch in Damon's inhale.

Micah now finally understands what the title means. That the connotation isn't perverted. There is simply a bond between them that implies safety, protection, and most importantly, a sign that Micah's needs will always be put first. Something that he has never once had the pleasure of experiencing, whether it be in life or the bedroom.

Damon's eyes roam over his face, the hand that rests against his cheek moves to the back of his neck and squeezes it.

"Shit, Micah. I hate that it took me this long to find you, but my god, you were worth the fucking wait."

He is captivated by Daddy's confession, feeling wanted for who he is for the first time in his life. No lies. No faking. And although he can't say it out loud, he feels the same way, wishing he escaped and found Damon sooner.

"How 'bout I put some cream on that beautifully reddened ass of yours and then I can cook us some dinner?"

All Micah can do is nod as he accepts the kiss Daddy plants on the tip of his nose before he stands to collect the lotion.

Chapter 9
Daddy and Little

RACHEL O'ROURKE

"What's Daddy going to make me do today?" Micah asks in his room, with his outfit on, and teddy in hand.

This time, the words have no sarcasm to them. The stupidity he felt last weekend is only nipping at his heels, and the name slides right off his tongue so naturally that he doesn't feel the difference between using Daddy or Damon.

"Today, I want my Little One to write a letter to his younger self."

Micah groans.

"Now, now. You remember the rules."

"Yeah, but I figured I could at least play some video games first." He crosses his arms over his chest.

"Wow, only took you twenty minutes to threaten to throw a tantrum."

"Pfft. You want to see a tantrum, I can give you a fuckin—" He stops, the smirk on Daddy's face makes it seem like he just won a bet. "Come on, I should at least get one pass each week since I need to ease back into this shit."

Daddy begins to chuckle. "Looks like you used your free pass and still broke the rule, Michelangelo."

Micah rolls his eyes.

"I want you to write thirty times, *Daddy's Little will not swear.*"

"But—"

"And then!" Daddy cuts him off. "I want at least a full page of you writing to your younger self. It can be about anything you want, but it has to be motivational. An encouragement about what you had; to what you now have."

"Gee, so freedom, acceptance. Seems pretty simple."

"Then it shouldn't take you that long to write it."

Daddy leans in and places a kiss on his forehead. It's the only place Daddy kisses him when he's in Little Space and yet it feels more intimate than when the man's tongue is down his throat.

Micah grumbles and mumbles as Daddy walks out, but a part of him sets out to prove that he can do this. That he doesn't want to disappoint.

"Knock, knock." Micah looks up to find Daddy at the door with a snack. "Ready for a break?"

"I just finished." He stays seated at the small table when he says, "You can come in, Daddy," and waits for the plate of fruit, cubed cheese, some crackers, and a few peanut butter M&M's.

"Here." Micah slides the thirty lines across to Daddy first, and then the letter, which he just finished reading over.

Daddy looks over the lines and gives an approving nod. "Good boy. Daddy's proud of you for accepting your punishment." But then pushes the letter back towards him. "But this isn't for me to read."

"Then why'd you ask me to write it?"

"Because it's to help you see how far you've come. Help you remember that you don't have to be that scared little boy anymore. That you can be yourself. It's a way for you to connect with your Little."

The salty peanut butter and sweet chocolate marinate in his mouth as he processes Daddy's words. He goes over in his head how he wrote to his younger self about being gay, and that he doesn't have to fight it like he did for so many years, just simply hide it to keep safe. He wrote about how to handle his parent's beliefs and lastly, although his younger self shouldn't have closed himself off from the world and those around him, it did allow him to open up just in time for the right person to step into his life, Damon.

"I have a surprise for you," Daddy says, interrupting his thoughts. When their eyes connect, the older man stands and opens the doors to all the games and activities and that's when Micah sees it.

"Is that?" His mouth is open, shocked at the sight.

"Surprisingly, it wasn't hard to find."

Micah stands, knowing that finding the vintage Lego pirate ship is easy, but it's the cost that would have been outrageous. Collectors hoard it until someone who desperately wants it comes along and pays anything to have it.

"I can't. Dam—*Daddy*, it's too much."

"I want my Little One to have it. I know how much it means to you and I know how much you'll enjoy building it." Micah's body is itching to step forward and touch the box, to look at the pictures and turn it in his hands before he rips it open to build.

"Michelangelo."

He turns to the sound of his name being whispered into the room.

"It would make Daddy very happy for you to have this gift…please."

How can he say no to that?

Micah swallows, then steps forward and accepts the gift, his hands shaking as he takes the box, holding it as though it's worth a million dollars.

A kiss is planted on his forehead. "Have fun my Little One. You deserve it." With a warm smile on Daddy's face, he walks out of the room, and Micah is left looking at the box in his hands.

It's a three-thousand-piece set, and Micah is only halfway when he senses eyes watching him. He follows the invisible gaze and finds Daddy smiling at the doorway.

"Having fun?"

"Yeah." A smile spreads across Micah's face. "Though considering the box says eight years and up, some of these instructions are complicated as fu—hell." He can't help but chuckle at the way he makes Daddy shake his head in disappointment while still smiling that heartwarming grin.

"Michelangelo, do I need to spank you each time you swear?"

The idea sounds more desirable than it does a punishment and it must show on his face.

"Of course, you'd see that as fun. I should know by now that my Little One can be a little devil."

Micah looks down and continues to build.

"It's dinner time, Michelangelo."

That must be why Daddy is at the door. "Already?"

"Yes. I've made a pasta bake and salad."

That alone causes Micah's stomach to grumble, but he doesn't want to break focus.

"Just one more hour. I can reheat the food but I'm so close to finishing."

"*Michelangelo.*"

"Pleassssse, Daddy." *Wow, since when does he beg?* Micah's never done that once in his entire life. At least not after his parents told him begging is for weak-minded people.

"How about this." Despite the back and forth, Daddy is still standing at the door, respecting Micah's space since he has not granted permission to enter. "We eat dinner and then you can come back and finish, doesn't matter how long it takes."

"For real?" He beams.

"Of course."

Micah stands, making sure everything is in place, so he knows exactly where he's up to before leaving the small wooden table and walking towards the door.

"Thank you, Daddy." As though his body is expecting it, Micah closes his eyes before Daddy's lips land on his forehead.

It's close to eight-thirty by the time his ship is complete. Micah marvels at its beauty. The process was extremely relaxing, his mind calm while he focused only on which piece went where, rather than the noise in his head, which he typically hears the day before work.

"That's beautiful, Michelangelo."

He takes his eyes off the ship so he can lay them on Daddy.

"Thanks. Probably wouldn't have been able to make it had I gotten the set when I was a kid."

"Oh, I doubt that very much."

This whole accepting of compliments is still hard for Micah to handle.

"You can come in. It's past seven, so…"

"Thank you." Daddy steps into the room. "But regardless, I still want to respect your space. Even if you're done being a Little for the day."

Micah begins to gnaw on his bottom lip. "What if I wanted it a little longer?" He speaks so softly that he isn't sure if Daddy heard him.

"Michelangelo, look at me, please." Daddy's voice is demanding but not cruel. Once their eyes lock, Daddy continues. "Where is your teddy?"

His soft bear is sitting on one of the wooden chairs beside Micah, and on instinct, he picks it up.

"Do you remember what I told you?"

Although he gives Daddy a nod, he still voices the words, "Whenever you see me holding him, you'll be here for whatever I need."

Daddy nods. "I see you holding him, Michelangelo. What do you need from Daddy?"

All day, his ass has had a lovely, dull ache each time he moved on the chair. Daddy even supplied a cushion, so he wasn't sitting directly on the hard wooden surface.

Micah wasn't exactly horny, though the memory of each and every spank flooded his mind when a twinge or a sting throbbed his cheeks, causing his dick to twitch once or twice. But what his body is seeking is unexpected, which is why he is finding it hard to use his voice to ask.

"You know whatever you say, Daddy will never laugh or get angry."

The soft fabric of his teddy takes away some of his nervous energy. It almost feels silky, which reminds Micah of Daddy's twenty-thousand thread count sheets.

Do sheets go that high? He doesn't know but God, they are soft.

"I, ah, I kinda liked how last week we watched a movie." He leaves out the part about cuddling, hoping it's implied. He looks up at Daddy, who has sunk back in the chair opposite him, shoulders relaxing and face softening once Micah begins to speak. "But now that the time is…I guess…"

"Michelangelo. Did you want to watch a movie with Daddy? Is that what it is?"

He exhales, relieved that Daddy can piece together what he is indirectly asking.

"Yes please, Daddy."

The proud smile of adoration on Daddy's face causes Micah's heart to beat faster, his cheeks to redden, and he feels proud of making his Daddy happy.

"Pick a movie and I'll even let you select something PG-13." Daddy winks before he stands, leaving him to set things up.

Ten minutes later, Daddy returns with a tray of snacks and drinks, placing it on a table to the side. Daddy sits down, and only once comfortable does his handsome man motion for Micah to join.

"What are we watching tonight?"

"Gremlins." Micah snuggles in so his body is resting against Daddy's side, a position that easily allows him to rest his head on Daddy's chest. "One night, it was on TV, and I was sitting on the floor watching it, excited to see a movie all my school friends were talking about." He reaches for his teddy to join them on the fluffy, extra-large beanbag. "I remember Gizmo had just been brought home when my parents walked in and told me I should be asleep. They kicked me out, and shamed me for staying up past bedtime. So, I never got to watch the rest. Never tried to either…"

Daddy moves a stray hair off Micah's forehead as he says, "If I recall, this movie can get a little scary. They even had to change the rating because of it. Think you can handle it, Little One?"

"Guess we'll find out. But just in case, it's a good thing Daddy's here to keep me safe." And there it is again, the sparkle in those magical green eyes, with a smile so broad it's almost from ear to ear.

Micah spent years only caring about himself because he knew no one else would. No one would accept him, look out for him and give him the life he wanted. It's why he stopped caring about what others thought once he knew none of those people would be there for him if he needed it, not once they knew he was gay. But when he does something that makes Damon happy, a swell of pride and satisfaction washes over him and it feels better than anything he's ever done that only benefited himself.

The movie starts.

"Would you like a Twizzler, Little One?"

"Yes please, Daddy." Micah goes to hold his hand out.

"Nuh-uh. Relax. Let Daddy feed you."

He automatically opens his mouth just enough for the rubbery red candy to be placed between his teeth. Micah bites down and begins to chew, his head resting on Daddy's chest.

Memories that he had long ago forgotten have slowly been seeping their way back as he's been spending time in Little Space. Emotions he pushed down, fears and excitement he remembers living. Damon is right—his childhood moulded who he became as an adult, but what if he doesn't have to be that person anymore?

Fingers begin to play with his hair, massaging his scalp. It's intimate what they are doing, how they are sitting, but Micah knows no sexual advances are going to be made and that in itself is freeing.

To be able to simply be held during a movie, to feel safe and protected for the first time in his life.

Chapter 10
Time Apart Makes the Heart Grow Fonder

Micah finds himself in a routine that fulfils every part of his mind, body, and soul. He works Monday to Friday, and during his time at the store, he thinks about Daddy, messages Daddy, or occasionally talks about him to the store owner when she looks up from her daily soap opera and cooking shows.

Friday nights, he goes back to his apartment and gives himself the longest shower of his life with a deep clean that he suspects reaches right into his stomach before heading over to Daddy's where he spends the entirety of his weekend.

On a few occasions, he leaves Daddy's bed Monday morning and makes the commute from the penthouse apartment to work, which starts his week off in a slightly more enjoyable way. It's rare, but Micah finds himself wanting to stay in Little Space longer than the set time they had agreed on. He begins to crave the headspace that allows him to let go of all adult responsibility and get lost in creative outlets that he was never allowed to do as a child.

It doesn't take long for him to realise he loves to draw. All the characters and creatures he's read in books are the inspiration behind each new piece. He finds himself inviting Daddy into his space, even if it's just for him to sit and read or work while Micah sketches out his drawings.

He follows the rules of writing a letter each week, sometimes to his younger self, and sometimes to the person he is today. Sometimes Daddy gives him a topic to write about, like a memory; good or bad, a dream or even an accomplishment.

He loves any activity that involves using his hands and mind. Lego. Colouring books. Blocks and puzzles. Through their conversations, he is no longer surprised to wake up each Sunday to a new gift from Daddy. An extra-large baggy T-shirt with Gizmo printed on the front. A first-edition novel by an author he had made a passing comment about after coming across their books at work. The highest quality pencils, oil pastels, and markers along with games and treats from memories long, long ago.

He comes to terms with accepting Daddy's desire to spend money on him, though he only asks that it's during their time together. Outside of the weekend, he can take care of himself and wishes to keep it that way.

But that doesn't mean, on occasion, when he's been texting Daddy, bitching about what a long shitty day he's had, he would arrive at his apartment to find Uber Eats waiting for him. Sometimes, it is a meal from a five-star restaurant that doesn't even offer delivery, yet one night, there stood a waiter, holding a signature dish that Daddy remembered to be one of his favourites.

They had begun to venture out, sharing a meal in public before partaking in their scheduled plans. It seems Daddy was taking notes on what Micah orders, enjoys and dislikes from the various menus.

Slowly, unaware that it's happening, his eating habits begin to change as well. Breakfast is more than just a coffee and a Pop-Tart. His lunch is now a protein with some form of rabbit food beside it and at dinner, he takes the time to cook himself a meal rather than place something in the microwave for five minutes.

None of it compares to the flavours Daddy easily creates and he still indulges in a pizza when he knows he has no plans to see his Daddy over the next day or two. With those changes in his diet, his body begins to thank him. He's sleeping better, lasts longer during sex, and can even bend and stretch in ways he never knew were possible while Daddy pounds into his hole and milks his prostate over and over again.

His ass builds up a tolerance to all the spanking, which allows him to melt into the heat and savour the sting for a longer period before he has to call it quits. Some days, he takes more rounds than others, but it never fails to amaze him how at the end of each Saturday, he's refreshed, settled and relaxed in a way that makes him feel like he could conquer the world.

Damon still attends the club, but it is strictly for business. From time to time, Daddy asks if Micah wants to accompany him. His answer is always the same: 'One day.' It's not that he doesn't want to go, he just wants to be ready to have everyone see him as Daddy's. He wants to be perfect with how he presents himself so Daddy is proud to show him off.

That was the point, after all.

A chance for Damon to announce to the patrons that he has a Sub, a Little. That he is taken, to an extent. Because there is no other reason for him to attend. His needs are being met and he trusts wholeheartedly that Damon isn't playing when he attends, so it isn't as though going is a chance for Micah to keep an eye on what is *his*.

It surprises Micah how easily trust has formed between them. Damon proves himself further by wearing a thin leather cuff bracelet to the club that not only has the symbol for 'master' attached to it, but also has his initials engraved on one side of the leather, with Damon's initials on the other. To an outsider, this would mean nothing, it has no recognisable power, but to Micah, it speaks volumes. Besides, Daddy spends most of the time sending him flirtatious messages that have a reply time so quick he knows his Daddy's mind could only be on him, not what is happening at the club.

The sex is earth-shattering. Their bodies mould together to become one, and their scents mix as sweat drips down them. Tongues lick and teeth mark. When Little Space finishes for the day, he, at times, initiates sex. His desire to be taken and owned in a way much different to how he spends his day bubbles to the surface and Daddy never refuses his advances. Test results are no longer required. They both know that no one besides each other is in the picture. Not once does Micah doubt Damon's loyalty, and to get to this level of their relationship feels rewarding.

Like a flick of a switch, Micah watches as his Daddy slips from his role as a caretaker and a loving father figure to an animalistic sex machine that can get him to unravel and come undone within minutes. It isn't Little Space that turns him on, it's the way he feels the devotion radiate off of Daddy, something he has never felt from a lover or a partner.

He believes the other reason why his libido kicks in after Little Space is due to his relaxed state of mind and the calm he always feels when leaving that space. With the lack of chaos in his head, he can focus his energy elsewhere.

At times, a playful side of himself appears, a brat, as his Daddy calls it, making Daddy work harder for sex, begging or grovelling to take what is his. Sometimes he turns their Saturdays into a day of chase, and once caught, only then does he get a spanking.

It is a power play.

He is always in control. But it is a chance for him to *feel it* rather than simply know it.

***

Six months into their contract, Micah is due to arrive any minute for their Friday night scheduling, but the moron on the phone has Damon preoccupied.

Why pay for a team to handle things if they are too stupid to get shit done?

Damon begins to argue back, explaining that the incident that took place in one of his clubs can't be ignored or brushed under the rug. The ding of his penthouse elevator registers in his ear, but his pacing prevents him from being able to stop and soak in the beauty of the man who has consumed his every waking thought over the last few months.

"No. That's unacceptable. This fuckhead knew the policy I had in place, and he thought he could undermine me and change the rules? Now look at the mess we're in because of his so-called management decision."

Damon's body is tense. He's going to have to fix this shit in person, but the thought of leaving Micah and spending time apart for the first time has him unsettled.

Arms suddenly encase Damon in a tight embrace that has the tension seeping out of his bones. His muscles relax and his body moulds into the only person who would be holding him, Micah. A deep sigh of contentment falls from Damon's lips as Micah lays his cheek against his back. With their height difference, Micah reaches his shoulder and yet, at that moment, Damon feels smaller. The phone conversation continues but he places his hand over Micah's, a silent thank you for the calming touch.

Eventually, his team agrees on what measures need to be taken. Pocketing his phone, he turns around, facing Micah for the first time that evening as they envelop one another.

"I had plans to take you to a restaurant tonight," he speaks into the crook of Micah's neck, taking a deep breath and having the scent of his Little One calm him.

"Had? What's changed?"

"I now have to get on a plane and deal with a mess at one of my clubs."

Micah pulls away, looking shell-shocked. Damon wishes he had the time to help him process the change to their plans but instead begins to collect various items around him before making a beeline for his bedroom.

"When is your flight?" Micah calls out to him.

"My jet is being prepared now. Shouldn't take me long to get to the airstrip."

"Wait." Suddenly Micah is standing at the bedroom door, eyes on the garment bag Damon has laid out, a variety of button-up shirts and suit jackets already inside. "You have a jet?"

Damon stops, a little hurt that Micah's focus isn't on the fact he has to leave but more so on his method of transport.

"It was left to me. I mostly lease it out. I don't generally travel much these days, at least not alone."

Much like the way a Submissive becomes dependent on a Dominant, Damon has become accustomed to his weekends with Micah. He is adamant that no one interrupts him from Friday evening until Monday morning. Their time together is limited, valued, and the Dominant inside him needs all that time to let loose and harness the control it craves.

"How long will you be gone for?" Micah's tone has changed to something with more uncertainty.

"Not sure. A week, maybe two. Some new manager went above my head and changed the rules on how things operate, which led to a fight breaking out in the middle of the club. Two people are in hospital with a concussion and being that I'm the higher majority owner, I now have to step in and sort this shit out, as well as fire the asshole for thinking my rules were worth ignoring."

They've gone days without seeing each other, and although they speak daily, there is a voice in Damon's head trying to plant doubt. Whispers that this is a chance for Micah to see that he might not need Damon as much as Damon needs Micah. This is why he craves being in control. The balance it gives him and the blanket of silence it throws over the negative voices in his head. As well as the doubts that any Dominant can have about themselves and their relationship with their Submissive.

It isn't even about the sex, the glorious spankings, or the cuddle sessions when he sits with his Little One. It's about the company he's about to lose. The solitude of his everyday life is about to continue for the next fourteen days.

He pushes it all down, zips up his bag, and walks toward Micah.

"I'm sorry I have to leave so quickly. I have been looking forward to tonight…to the weekend. I practically count down the days the minute I wake up Monday morning." He speaks the truth like he had always promised, wanting Micah to know that had there been a choice, he would have chosen him. "Stay here while I'm gone."

Micah's hazel eyes widen in surprise.

"Please. You can enjoy time in your room if you need it. Build, colour. I'll even allow you to have more than two hours of screen time to make up for my absence and no letter this week." He's close to begging. But at least this way, he knows where Micah is, and what he's doing, giving him a small sense of control while away.

Micah's eyes dart around the room, perhaps looking for an answer. Damon settles his baby's racing mind by placing his thumb and index finger on Micah's chin, forcing their eyes to meet.

"The thought of you sleeping in my bed, maybe even playing in it while I'm gone...well," his voice drops, "the visuals alone will keep me company while I'm away from you." He seals his words with a kiss, a promise of sorts.

With a contented sigh, their lips part, but he never lets go of Micah's chin.

"Stay," Damon whispers against angelic lips. "I'll organise food for you, so you won't have to lift a finger."

"If this is what you want, Daddy, then I'll stay." Micah looks down, making himself appear shy and vulnerable. Damon feels feral and possessive every time he sees it. The alpha male inside of him wants to protect what's his. Once again, he raises Micah's chin so he's no longer looking at the floor.

"What *I* want is to sink into that tight little hole of yours like a man who's been locked behind bars for a decade," he purrs. "What *I want*, is to leave my mark on your ass from each smack of my hand. But most of all, what I want," his voice softens, "is to take care of my Little One, and make sure he is feeling appreciated and cared for."

Damon notices heat rise to Micah's cheeks.

"Did I make you blush, Michelangelo?" It's rare to use Micah's full name outside of Little Space, but the mix of all three worlds that they partake in is the rush he needs before jet-setting off.

"I'll stay. And I promise to dirty the sheets," Micah bites his bottom lip, "and wear your clothes and watch movies with a rating well above the parental guide."

"I'll order you food from the car. Have fun, baby. Whatever you want, it's yours."

With a kiss goodbye, he slips out of his role as Daddy and back into the life of Damon Stone, CEO. With his phone and bag in hand, he walks out, not looking back, knowing he wouldn't be able to leave if he did.

***

Sleeping alone in Daddy's bed feels foreign, as though he shouldn't be here. A delicious Italian feast was delivered to the penthouse. More food than Micah could eat on his own, which only reminded him that the meal was meant to be shared with Daddy.

Once sex began to happen outside of their scheduled Friday nights, they sometimes decided to eat afterwards so they could swap the lighter meals for something heartier. Around the same time, they also expanded to restaurants for their meals rather than homemade by Daddy. It allowed for morning sex before a day of spanking, or a roll in the sheets after Little Space before parting for the night. And sometimes, on a Monday morning, when Micah stayed the whole weekend, he was rewarded with a quickie.

He can't blame his lack of orgasm for his inability to sleep. He used one of the toys under the bed to get himself off, sending a few photos to Daddy, proving that he obeyed orders. With a sigh of frustration, he reaches for his phone.

Micah

I can't sleep, Daddy.

Three dancing dots appear. Considering the hour, he is surprised Daddy is awake.

Daddy

> What's on your mind, baby?

> Bed is too big. And cold. You should be here.

It may be selfish of him to prioritise his needs and wants over Damon's work, but this is the first time their plans together have been cancelled, leaving him feeling uneasy from the change in routine.

> I wish I were there. Holding you. Kissing you. Touching you.

Micah closes his eyes momentarily, envisioning Daddy doing all those things.

> Try and get some sleep, baby. I promise I won't be gone for long. I'll call you once I land.

> You're still flying? How are you messaging me?

> Private jets have phone service. Don't worry, I wasn't going to make it so you couldn't contact me. Now sleep, that's an order. xx

Throwing his phone to the opposite side of the bed, he rolls over and wraps himself around a pillow. It's his Daddy's pillow, and the scent and comfort lull him to sleep, proving that it may have been all that he needed.

He spends Saturday in the library. It's the only way he can think to pass the time, and it helps distract his mind from the lack of heat and tenderness his ass would normally be feeling. The day moves quickly as he immerses himself in another world, only stopping when the phone connected to the doorman below rings, alerting him to a food delivery.

Daddy keeps his promise by sending three meals a day to the penthouse, making sure Micah doesn't have to lift a finger.

It's after he has finished dinner that another call from below interrupts his book. This time, Micah isn't sure what the delivery could be, seeing how his dinner came with a side of dessert and late-night snacks.

With excitement and caution, he opens the box once the doorman has taken the elevator back downstairs. Inside, he finds a grey otter plush, roughly fifteen inches long and softer than his teddy, which almost seems impossible.

"Okaaaaaaaay." He studies the otter, curious as to why Daddy sent it to him. Right on cue, his phone rings with Daddy's name proudly displayed on the screen.

"Did it arrive?" Daddy's voice comes through the speaker, no hello, but a sense of pride in his tone.

"*It* did." He turns the plush around, trying to see if there is a note or instructions on it.

Daddy's chuckle echoes through the phone. "See the heart on its stomach?"

He spots it. "Yeah."

"Press it." Doing as he's told, the light grey stomach lights up with a warm yellow hue. The otter begins to move, its stomach pushing in and out, mimicking the way a person's chest moves when breathing, and only then does he hear the sound.

Inhaling and exhaling.

Soft, calming breaths that sound exactly like—

"It's called a breathing buddy. They are designed to help with relaxation, comfort and separation anxiety."

"How does it sound just like you?"

"Your mind is taking comfort in what you want it to sound like, what it needs to hear. And if you don't want the breathing, it has calming music."

"*Daddy.*" He can't understand why his body has a sudden urge to cry. "This is so stupid." He sniffs back tears. "It's not like I go days without seeing you. Why is this hitting me so hard?"

"The routines and habits that we create give us a sense of safety. You built that through Little Space but also by trusting me and inviting me into your world…your life. You, as always, were in control of when we saw each other, even if it happened outside of our scheduled weekend. But I took some of that control away when I left. I was the one that changed your routine, and it's created this insecurity inside of you."

"You make it sound like I'm reliant on you."

"I mean, in some ways, you are, but not in a way that makes you fragile or powerless. The routine we created is designed to help reduce your stress, your need to constantly make decisions, and to fulfil a deeper desire that can't be found in a standard relationship."

Relationship?

"I can't promise it will get easier, but I promise to find ways to make it less stressful. Starting with your breathing buddy."

Sniffing back tears, Micah holds the otter close, the sensation of its chest breathing against his is already helping with the ache inside of him.

"Thank you, Daddy."

"You're welcome, Little One." Although he isn't in Little Space, the name brings a soothing comfort, as that part of him is also under stress. The separation from Daddy affects all versions of himself.

"Why an otter?"

"When sea otters sleep, they hold hands, so they don't drift apart. I thought it would be a nice reminder that regardless of how far apart we are, I'll always be beside you, holding your hand, making sure you don't drift away without me."

During Daddy's explanation, Micah had made his way into the bedroom, the phone still to his ear, with his new plush breathing in his arms. His body is suddenly exhausted.

"'m gonna go to sleep now, Daddy."

"Good boy. Rest. I'll call you tomorrow."

"'ove you." The words slip out, his relaxed mind making it easier to be honest. As he floats in and out of consciousness, what Micah knows for certain is the sound of Daddy saying, "Love you, too," just before he drifts off to sleep.

LITTLE ONE

A day in Little Space after a solid night's rest is the best way to end the weekend. Micah colours in a drawing of a torso tied in shibari and builds a tower with his Lego. He watches a Star Wars movie and then makes a racetrack for his toy cars.

He stops for meals, once again ordered and delivered by Daddy who calls him towards the end of the day, around the time he slips out of Little Space and is deciding whether to stay or go home for the evening.

"How was your day, Little One?"

"Fun. You missed out on the tower I built. Almost as tall as me."

"I'm sorry Daddy missed that. Can you build it for me again when I get home?"

"Hmmm, maybe. What do I get if I do?" The playful side of him seems to linger.

"Is my Little One being cheeky?"

"Maybe. Not like you're here to punish me."

"Oh, Michelangelo. Don't underestimate my power just because I'm not there."

"That so?" he challenges. There is no reply for a minute, a smile forming on Micah's face as he thinks he has won, only for the TV to shut off suddenly.

"In case you're wondering," Daddy's voice breaks the silence, "all the electronics in the house are now locked. No TV, gaming, or music."

"You—how? What?"

"I said that you could take it easy today, that doesn't mean you can be rude and forget your manners. Daddy's Little One is well-behaved and appreciative, not spoilt."

Micah stands there, flabbergasted, though the notion is short-lived once the realisation of what just happened sets in. Regardless of distance, Daddy still has control, and the small punishment Micah is now facing only reminds him that they are still in their respective roles.

"I'm sorry, Daddy. Was only teasing because I miss you so much."

"I miss you too. But I'm still not unlocking the devices. At least not until after dinner."

"Any chance dinner is you?" He steps out of his room, out of Little Space and walks into the bedroom to change into sweats and a hoodie.

"Afraid not. As I had suspected, this mess is going to take a couple of weeks."

Micah groans.

"I know, baby. I don't like it either." There is a pause. "Stay at my place."

"Tonight?"

"Yes, but also until I return. Stay so I know you're okay. So I can take care of you. I'll have dinner ready for you after work and breakfast delivered when you wake up."

"I don't know." The offer sounds nice in theory, but apart from the fact that he can leave and go to work, the idea has him feeling like a kept boy.

"Micah," Daddy's voice drops. "Don't make Daddy beg."

He gulps. His cock twitches from the husky deep tone.

"The choice is yours. Always. But I won't lie, the thought of you making yourself at home in my penthouse while we're apart does bring me joy."

A soft voice in his head stops him from overthinking. *This is how Daddy is showing his love.*

Wait, love?

The memory comes fading back; *"'ove you." "Love you, too."*

Oh fuck.

A wave of panic begins to wash over him like a tidal rising.

"Micah?"

How long has Damon been calling his name?

"You don't have to panic, Micah. I can hear your mind ticking away from the other side of the country."

"I—last night, we—"

"It's okay. The word love can be used in all different variations." It never ceases to amaze him how well Daddy can decipher his fears and thoughts. "Such as the love between child and parent. Between friends. There can be love between a Dominant and a Submissive without it suggesting that either wants to be in a romantic relationship."

"It can?"

"Of course. But Micah, this contract has no end date. And as much as it pains me to know you may one day decide to go, know that you can decide that day whenever you wish, for whatever reason."

Is Damon suggesting that he can leave if he finds himself falling in love with him?

"If we stopped, would I ever see you again?"

There is a pause. "For a period, no. It would be best to keep a distance until we adjusted to functioning without the other. It can be a shock to the system. Your mind and body have been so reliant on our dynamic. But if or when that time comes, I would like to think our time together has given you the tools to know what your body wants, what it needs, and how to understand it when it's time to give it those desires. But, after some time, if we were both free, we could play from time to time, similar to the night we met."

Flashes of that kid on Damon's lap come to mind and the image makes his stomach churn. He pushes the bile down, along with the memory, and reminds himself that Damon has been his, exclusively, for six months.

"Thank you for explaining it." It's all he can bring himself to say. "And I'll think about it…your offer. I'll stay tonight and see how I feel in the morning."

"That's all I ask."

"Besides, I'm going to need to go home to get clothes."

"You could…or I can have a new wardrobe delivered tomorrow morning for you to keep at my place for moments like this."

"Daddy." This time he is the one to drop his tone.

"What did I say about not questioning my monetary decisions?"

"And what did I say about spending money on me outside of the weekend?"

"Technically, it's only eight o'clock."

"Damon," he warns.

"Get some rest. You have work tomorrow."

The phone disconnects. He stares at the black screen, knowing without a doubt that he will wake up to the arrival of shopping bags with clothes that equal the cost of his whole apartment.

With a deep breath, Micah decides not to fight it. It's Damon's money, after all. If he wants to waste it on him, so be it. He can at least take some pride in knowing that he hasn't asked for any of these things.

A series of beeps go off in the penthouse. Alarmed at first that something is wrong, he looks around, only to realise the lock on the devices has been removed. Although he has had a chill day, new thoughts now rummage through his head. Thoughts centred around the word *love*, contract end dates, and what life would be like when this is all over.

The last one has his heart racing and exhaustion creeps back in. It's too early to sleep, but he's not against lying in bed, with his breathing otter snuggled beside him. He'll leave these decisions for another day.

Chapter 11

Reward

RACHEL O'ROURKE

After two long, mundane weeks, Daddy messages him during his lunch break, confirming that he has arrived home and will be waiting for him that evening with a surprise. Micah hopes it's a hard nine inches. He is no stranger to going without sex for months, but Micah now feels like an addict, itching for that next hit since he's been receiving it on the regular.

Using the keycard Daddy gave him so that he no longer needs to rely on the doorman to grant him access, the elevator doors open onto the penthouse floor, and Micah steps into darkness. Not even the city lights can be seen thanks to the drawn blackout blinds.

As his eyes adjust, he spots a small floor lamp illuminating a pathway to the bedroom. Micah follows the same way Dorothy did the yellow brick road. In the bedroom, he is met with a chair, a note, and what appears to be an item of clothing. But no Damon.

Get changed. Put on the blindfold and sit.
Daddy wants to play.

By change, Daddy means stripping down to nothing but lace panties that feel like silk against his skin. He's never worn lingerie. Never thought about it let alone wanted to, though it is something they have spoken about. Discussed whether Micah would ever consider the idea. And since tonight is about Daddy's desires, and finally connecting after two weeks away from him, he is willing to agree to anything.

Once Micah slips the blindfold on and takes a seat on the chair, his senses heighten. Without the ability to see, he can hear the soft footsteps of bare feet on the carpet. His nose instantly picks up on the cologne he knows to be his Daddy's, and as fingertips gently brush down Micah's arm, goosebumps litter his skin from how sensitive he is to the touch.

"Can you see me?" his Daddy asks.

"No." The word is faint.

"No, what?"

"No, Daddy."

"That's better, baby." Lips peck at his neck, leaving a trail from his ear down his collar, and stopping to lick and nip at his nipples.

"You look beautiful in your new outfit. How does it feel?"

"Sexy…naughty…" His hands are gently pulled behind his back, and a satin rope ties them together behind the chair.

"Colour?"

"Green!"

"Mmmm," Daddy purrs into his ear. "Do you want to know what I think of your new outfit?"

"Yes, Daddy."

"I think you look like a good boy who did exactly what Daddy asked while he was away and *now*, you deserve a reward."

The anticipation has Micah panting.

"Open that pretty mouth and show me that tongue."

He follows Daddy's orders. *God*, this is invigorating. Just when he thinks it can't get any more tantalising, Daddy's thumb enters his mouth roughly, deep, nearly gagging him. But he holds his own, proving he can take it.

"Suck."

Micah doesn't have to be asked twice. He puts his tongue to work, swirling around Daddy's thumb, licking the tip and swallowing it down to the knuckle, giving a taste of what's to come when his true reward is put inside his mouth.

"Good boy, get it nice and wet for Daddy." Saliva dribbles down Micah's chin when the thumb is removed from his mouth. The pad of Daddy's finger drags over his lips, lathering them with his spit.

"If it becomes too much, stomp your foot twice. Three times to stop. Do you understand me?"

"Yes, Daddy."

"Repeat it."

"Twice to ease up. Three times to stop."

"God, you're beautiful when you listen."

Like a dog waiting for a bone, Micah opens his mouth, tilting his head back slightly to allow the ease of Daddy's cock to slide smoothly down his throat.

The weight of Daddy's nine inches is tapped against his tongue. Saliva pools in his mouth from the anticipation and saltiness of his reward.

"That's a good boy. Show Daddy how gorgeous that mouth of yours is."

Slowly, inch by inch, he takes Daddy's cock into his mouth, relaxing his jaw to allow easier access. He gags as the tip touches the back of his throat, but he doesn't stomp his foot. No. He holds on to the last bit of oxygen left in his lungs, and begins to bob back and forth.

"That's it. Prove to me how much you've missed this cock."

Micah hums and groans, sending a vibration up the length of Daddy's dick. His tongue trails up the shaft and as he mouths at Daddy's balls, the slap of a hard wet cock on his face makes his own strain in the fabric of his lace panties.

"Jesus, baby. Want to fuck that pretty little mouth of yours so badly."

"Do it. Please, Daddy. Wreck me."

"How can I say no with manners like that?"

While still unable to see, the firm grip on his hair lets Micah know his mouth is about to be ruined. This time, there is no taking it easy. His breath is ripped out of him as Daddy plunges down his throat. The thought of bruises already forming makes him even more cock-drunk than he already is. The gluck-gluck sound fills the room as his hair is yanked and his mouth is fucked within an inch of his life.

He's abruptly pulled off and he gasps for air.

"God, I missed you," Daddy pants before his lips crash onto Micah's swollen ones, tongues messy and sloppy before the kiss is broken too quickly.

Firm hands slide under Micah's thighs, clenching before they lift him from his perch on the chair. His arms, which are still tied together, glide over the chair's back, releasing him from his throne only to be placed on another.

Daddy drops him onto the mattress, his back bouncing against the springs.

"Open wide, want to see that black lace shimmer against your skin."

His legs fall open quicker than a whore's. He's hard, leaking. A wet patch has soaked through the lace, which he suspects Daddy has noticed when he hears a growl from above.

"Touch me, Daddy. *Pleeease*," he begs, aching to feel skin-on-skin, craving Daddy's tender touch. He's missed him so much.

"Shhh, we have all night to make up for lost time." Teeth scrape and lips kiss from his ankle up to his thigh. The closer Daddy gets to his dick, the more his body writhes and whimpers. His fingers clench the bedsheets, needing something to grab hold of, wishing it was his Daddy's back he was clawing at, leaving his mark.

"Oh, fuck!" he moans as Daddy takes him into his mouth, sucking him off through the lace fabric. "Yes, Daddy. Don't stop." His words have the opposite effect, it seems, as the pleasure stops, and the air has him hissing from the sudden cold.

"Are you telling me what to do?"

He whines, "No, Daddy."

"That's what I thought. Good boys know they should do as they're told and not make demands."

Biting his lip to avoid speaking out of line, Micah nods in agreement and waits patiently. He gasps when hands clamp onto his hips and flip him onto his stomach.

"Face down, ass up," Daddy instructs.

With his hands still tied, it's a challenge, but he manages to get his balance.

"Perfect."

Warm hands rub and squeeze his ass, the lace riding up as Daddy spreads his cheeks. "You're beautiful, Micah. Was so proud of you, the way you behaved when I was away. Listened and did as Daddy asked."

"Wanna make you happy."

"Oh, baby. You make me more than happy." At this point, the praise alone might be enough to get him off. "You're so special to me. After all this time, I'm still so crazy about you. That ass. That pout."

Spit lands on his hole. The shock has his body moving away, only for his ass to push back against the fingers that are rubbing up and down his perineum.

"Did you open yourself up before arriving tonight?"

"Yes, Daddy. As requested."

"Did you think of me when doing it?" Daddy's voice is sultry.

"Thought of your fingers inside of me." As he says it, Daddy's thumb pushes inside of him.

He moans.

"Keep going or I'll stop."

He tries to get his brain back online. "I-I thought of your tongue opening me up."

Daddy's thumb hooks into his rim, making room for the slither of a warm, wet tongue.

"Oh, *fuck!*" At this point, he considers saying anything if it means Daddy's going to recreate it.

"Then I thought about riding you into the mattress and proving to you how much I missed you."

Everything stops, and if it not for the panting breaths behind him, Micah could swear he's alone in the room.

"You want to ride this dick?"

"Yes, Daddy," he says with conviction, yet with an ache behind the words.

"You think you earned it?"

"Yes, Daddy."

"Why?"

"Because I did as Daddy asked…and because it's mine."

The bed dips. Micah's face is still pressed against the mattress until he's suddenly manhandled onto a warm, toned body. He kneels, placing a leg on either side of Daddy's hips, and a hard, leaking cock presses against his ass.

"Damn straight it's yours."

The lace panties are pulled to the side rather than removed, and the sound of a cap popping off indicates that lube is being applied. He waits patiently, though it's only a façade, masking how badly the voice inside of him is begging to be filled.

With his hands still tied, he relies on Daddy to line himself up. He feels the tip nudging at his entrance, as though it's asking for permission to come in. Micah grants it by slowly lowering himself down, his head tilting back as he basks in the stretch.

"Take it, baby. I know you can."

He sinks onto the full length, bottoming out, panting from already feeling so full.

"Now ride."

Micah doesn't give himself time to adjust. With giant hands gripping his thighs for support, he begins to rock back and forth. He's positive he can feel Daddy in his stomach, claiming him from the inside out.

"If only you could see yourself right now." Daddy's hands trail from his thighs to his hips. Squeezing. Marking. Claiming.

The drag against his walls is euphoric. His plump ass ripples as he moves and the sound of his cock slapping against his stomach can be heard over their moans.

It's not enough though. He needs the tickle of that sweet spot inside of him. Switching techniques, Micah begins to bounce on Daddy's dick like a pogo stick. His thighs burn, but on the second squat, electricity shoots up his spine.

"Holy fuck. Right there, Daddy." His skin is glistening with sweat, risking the blindfold slipping from his eyes, but he doesn't let up. He chases his orgasm, losing himself to the constant pounding of his prostate. His hard tip leaks with the need to come.

"'m close, Daddy."

When Daddy's hand wraps around his shaft, he doesn't even have to move for his cock to release thick white strings of cum onto Daddy's chest. Marking him as his.

"God, yes. Cover me, baby. Want to be painted in your cum," Daddy orders, his body now taking control and thrusting into his used hole, chasing his release as Daddy shudders and slows down above him.

The blindfold is ripped from his eyes. The room is dark, but a halo of light illuminates the room, helping him adjust quickly. Daddy looks wrecked, feral from the need to come. Damon's legs plant firmly into the mattress and cling to Micah like a lion clawing into its prey.

Micah leans forward, burying his head into the crook of Daddy's neck, who thrusts into him like a jackhammer. Micah's teeth graze Daddy's collarbone, fingers dig into Micah's back, and then, without warning, cum shoots inside of him, filling him to the brim. Daddy holds still, using his cock as a plug to make sure every drop stays inside of him.

Secure arms hold Micah tight while his body weight soothes Daddy. Legs tremble beneath Micah as Daddy groans and huffs.

"You were amazing, baby…you're always amazing," Daddy whispers into his ear as Micah trembles with pride and the come-down from his body's overstimulation. Daddy removes the silk ties from his wrists, but Micah keeps his arms in place, waiting for Daddy to rub at his skin and muscles, loosening them to avoid any cramping.

"Are you okay?"

Micah nods, his head still resting on Daddy's shoulder. "Missed you, is all."

"Missed you too."

They stay like that until Micah makes the first move to get up and get cleaned. Their loving embrace is aftercare in itself.

With sex taking priority before dinner, they can now indulge in an assortment of dishes from the local Thai restaurant not far from Daddy's penthouse. Sitting on the rug in the living room, Daddy wears nothing but low-riding cashmere sweatpants, V-lines deliciously on display, while Micah settles for a baggy T-shirt. The fireplace offers warmth and ambience as they eat. Chopsticks in hand, they take turns feeding themselves and each other, passing food back and forth while laughing and catching up on the time they were apart.

"Did you sort everything out or do you have to go back?" Micah asks.

"It's sorted. But in my line of work, these things can happen. Situations arise that involve me having to up and leave with no notice."

"Must be hard on your relationships." Micah keeps his eyes down, chopsticks digging around into the food.

"It can be. Especially in the early stages when I was setting myself up. Now, it doesn't happen as frequently. I have a trusted body of staff that I can rely on. However, I still need to show my face from time to time."

Micah nods, emotions he has never felt before simmering above the surface. Emotions that were dormant until he walked through those elevator doors and back into the arms of the man he loves.

There is no denying that he loves Damon, the man who has helped open his world. He spent the last two weeks living alone in the penthouse to reflect on everything that's changed. He also envisioned himself coming home after work to this apartment. To Damon.

He tried to picture himself being spanked by someone else, fucked by someone else. The thought alone made him nauseous, and he rushed to the bedroom and turned on his breathing buddy to help calm the anxiety that had built at the thought. Once settled, only then did he continue his daydream of playing house, for real, not just within the terms of their contract.

He can't deny that this level of love is romantic. Damon spoke of platonic love when away, a love built on caring and trusting someone, but this goes deeper than that…though he isn't sure how long he's felt this way.

"Maybe next time, you could come with me." Daddy's words bring him out of his thoughts. His head snaps up, and their eyes lock on one another.

"Really?"

"I wouldn't have suggested it had I not meant it."

"You're not just saying it because of what I said?"

"What you said?" The confusion on Daddy's face matches the tone of his voice.

"When I said I love you," he explains outright.

Daddy puts his food down, brushing his hands together to remove invisible crumbs.

"If I recall correctly, I said 'I love you, too,' did I not?"

"Y-yeah. But I thought maybe you were being polite."

"I don't do anything out of politeness. I speak the truth, that's what I told you."

"So, you love me?" He sounds surprised.

"Do you need me to say it again?"

He nods.

"I love you, Micah."

He wants to ask whether that love is as a Dominant or a partner, but the fear of learning which one it may be stops him.

"I guess next time, I could come." He changes the subject. "Though how would everyone know I'm yours?" He flirts to cover up the thumping of his heart.

"Hmmm, maybe I need to get you a pretty little collar for that gorgeous neck of yours."

On instinct, his hand comes up to his neck, wrapping around it as though he is touching the collar Daddy speaks of.

"I've never used a collar before," he admits, unsure how he feels about one.

"There are different types, all representing different statuses. There is the collar of consideration, a Dom would put it on a Submissive when they are starting out, testing to see if they are worthy of being their full-time Sub."

"So, when we started the contract, that's when I would have worn something like that?"

"Yes, if that was part of our scene. During our trial, I would have made sure you wore one." Micah nods, waiting for further examples.

"The training collar is used when a Dom has selected their Sub, but they need training and time to adjust to new rules, or perhaps they've never been a Submissive before. Then there is one for protection. These are much more serious."

"How so?"

"It means that the Dominant is taking responsibility for this person. It's a sign of ownership and can be used when a Submissive has been mistreated by a Dom, helping them adjust back into the scene of safe play. It can also be used for Submissives who need protection from themselves, perhaps they have been playing dangerously. Not using safe words where it's been needed—"

"Punishing themselves through self-destructive behaviour."

"Exactly."

It's fascinating how much time has passed since he and Daddy shared a similar conversation.

"Then you have play collars, which are used within a scene. Day collars for Submissives who want to step out and still feel owned. These are generally a little less conspicuous. And then lastly, the eternity collar."

"Eternity."

"The most serious of all. It's as serious as a wedding ring in the BDSM world as it's to be worn permanently. The Dom is the only one with the key. Removing it can be seen as the relationship ending, but in some cases, couples can negotiate when to wear it, and what might replace it when it's not worn."

"If you were to give me one right now, which would it be?

"A day collar." The answer is quick. "Whether it be a collar itself or a piece of jewellery, simply knowing you were walking around with a symbol of who you belong to around your neck, a sign that you're mine. Well, I couldn't think of anything more empowering and seductive."

They finish eating while Micah entertains the idea of chains, collars, and fine jewellery around his neck for the world to see.

Chapter 12
Testing the Boundaries

Going out for a meal as Damon and Micah is now second nature. However, going out as Daddy and Little One, they've yet to try. One Sunday morning, Daddy suggests going out to breakfast during Little Time. Had the idea been brought to the table five months ago, Micah would have declined, but now, eight months into their contract, he holds this confidence in himself and his kinks that have him agreeing.

Daddy takes him to the café they met at many moons ago to discuss their contract, and once again, Shannon is working and recognises them immediately. Shannon eyes him in his jeans—that are rubbing against his well-spanked ass—and a baggy hoodie that has a dinosaur on the front, with fabric-made spikes on the arms and a hood to make it look as though he is a stegosaurus.

Not a single ounce of him feels like an idiot or embarrassed to be seen in his outfit. Daddy told him to dress warm and the material is not only that, but it's soft against his skin, reminding him of the cuddle sessions he has every Sunday with his Daddy and will receive once they go back home after breakfast.

They sit inside due to the weather, the cafe somewhat busy, but with a glance, he notices what Damon was referring to when he said this location is a safe space for couples and play partners like themselves. He sees some people in collars, some with a leash attached to said collar. A few are in baby onesies and others are sitting directly on the laps of their Dominant while being fed or, in some cases, stroked like a cat. He even spots a tail or two when he looks hard enough.

During his time with Daddy, the older man has shared his knowledge, as well as the various kinks that Micah never would have known were a thing. Daddy has been teaching him while also broadening his mind. The world is already full of so much hate and judgement, and he doesn't want to be another added to that list. He wants to walk into a room and not be the only one gawking at what he doesn't understand, which is why he asks Daddy to help him.

Thanks to those discussions, as they sit for breakfast, nothing causes his jaw to drop to the floor, though this is still a family environment, meaning nothing is going to be X-rated.

Suddenly, something comes over him. An idea. A scene of sorts. It could be that they're in public, or because he is being a Little for the first time around others, but when breakfast is placed in front of them, he reaches for his chocolate milk, slurps half of it up the straw only so he can blow bubbles into his cup.

"Michelangelo, that's enough," Daddy instructs.

"But Daddy, it's fun," he replies coyly, fully aware that he's being rude and breaking the dining etiquette rules.

"And I said to stop it." Daddy's voice is stern.

He stops. But then he begins to enjoy his meal with nothing but his hands as he picks up the omelette with his fingers and tilts his head back to drop the eggs and vegetables down his throat.

Daddy stops eating, his cutlery dropping with frustration onto the table. "I'm not going to ask you again, Michelangelo."

He doesn't know what possesses him to behave in such a way. He doesn't like to upset Daddy and corner time or writing lines is never fun, but even with Daddy's final warning, he picks up what is left of his chocolate milk and blows a bubble so big that the milk spills over the edge and onto the table.

With more calmness than Micah thought possible, Daddy wipes his mouth with the cloth napkin he has lying across his lap and then rises from the table. He waits with bated breath.

"Please stand, Michelangelo."

He does.

"Does your bum hurt after last night's fun?"

He nods.

"Well, let's see how it feels sitting on a polished concrete floor while I finish my meal." And with that, Daddy moves him from behind the table and instructs him to sit on the floor beside Daddy's chair. Micah crosses his legs and the ache in his cheeks instantly reacts to his new perch. All he can tell himself is thankfully, Daddy doesn't have much food left on his plate.

But when Shannon comes to collect the plate, he is surprised to hear Daddy order a second Americano with a chocolate croissant. When she walks away, unphased by his position on the floor, Daddy speaks up, however, it isn't at him.

"Excuse me, everyone," Damon's voice booms through the cafe. "I'm sorry to interrupt your meals but it seems my Little One decided he wants to play with his food today rather than eat it. He knows better than that. Before you leave, you're welcome to stop by and offer him advice so that next time, he behaves."

Micah looks up at Daddy, surprised that his punishment isn't as simple as sitting by his feet like a disobedient child.

While Daddy drinks his coffee and eats his food, he keeps his eyes on the floor as others walk past and do as Damon suggested.

"That's very disappointing, Little One. You should show some respect."

"Your Daddy dotes on you, and this is how you repay him? How upsetting."

"If my Little One behaved like this he'd be pulled over my knee in front of everyone."

"Maybe you'll think twice before acting like a spoiled brat."

"However you're feeling right now, imagine how your Daddy is feeling. How disheartened he is."

"This hurts your Daddy more than it hurts you, Little One. Remember that."

A tear falls down his cheek, which he quickly wipes away before Daddy sees. However, that's the exact moment that strong arms lift him from his seated position on the floor, placing him on a warm, comforting lap.

"Oh, Michelangelo." Daddy's soft, nurturing voice opens up a floodgate of tears that he is unable to stop. "Please don't cry, my Little One."

Micah never cries. He hates it. His father said it was a sign of weakness and right now, it's only causing him to feel deeper emotions that he would rather repress.

"'M sor-sorry, Daddy." Daddy pushes his hair away from his forehead and wipes the tears from his cheek.

"I'm sorry too. They were right, you know, that hurt me just as much as it hurt you."

"I do-don't want to disappoint you." Once the words leave his mouth, more tears fall. He bows his head, too ashamed to look into Daddy's eyes.

Has he gone too far?

Is Damon going to end the contract?

Is he yet again a failure?

"Michelangelo…" A gentle hand softly grips the tip of his chin. He is not forced to look his Daddy in the eyes, but the energy from Daddy's fingers encourages him to do so. "Please, Little One. Look at Daddy."

When he looks into the eyes of the man he has learnt to trust and open himself up to more than anyone he has ever known, the world around him vanishes. He doesn't feel any other eyes on him except for Daddy's.

"You could never be a disappointment to me, Michelangelo. Do you hear me?"

It isn't until he gives a single nod that Daddy continues.

"You're exquisite, in every way. And you're perfect for me."

He searches Daddy's green eyes for a hint of a lie, but he doesn't see one.

"A physical punishment is not always the option. It takes a well-trained Dom who knows their partner well enough to understand the best form of punishment."

He sniffs.

"You grew up in a world where words hurt more than action, and you enjoy getting spanked from sunup to sundown." Daddy offers a slight smirk, which helps ease some of the tension. "That's why I knew a verbal punishment would help you learn your lesson."

"...The things those people said…"

"Hurt. Yes, I'm sure it did. When we are in public together, you represent me, Michelangelo. Your actions reflect who I am as your Dom, as your Daddy. And so, if what was said to you upset you, then subconsciously, you too regret your actions and how they reflected on me."

Micah doesn't speak.

"Michelangelo, do you know why you did that today? Why you tried to defy me? Why you wanted to play up?"

He didn't think he did.

He thought he was being a kid. But after those strangers directed their words at him, their disapproval like venom in his veins, he knows why he did it.

"I wanted to know…" He breaks eye contact. "I wanted to know how far I could go for you to *really* punish me…"

Daddy inhales deeply, then slowly exhales.

"I see." Daddy raises his hand, which is when Micah remembers they are still at the café.

"Shannon," Damon calls. "That will be all for today."

"Yes, sir. I'll charge it to your card on file," the waitress explains.

"Thank you."

Daddy moves him from his lap and into a standing position. The stretch of his skin causes his ass muscles to throb, but he can't enjoy it.

"Let's get you home." Daddy takes his hand as they walk out. With his head hung low, Micah looks around the room. No one is watching them. No one is whispering or staring. He raises his head slightly, trying to earn back some self-confidence.

***

Standing in Micah's room, Damon helps his Little One change into comfy 'Little' clothes that he's to wear when in play. They haven't said a word to each other since leaving the café. They sit on the cream-coloured loveseat that is large enough for them both to cuddle on. It was a gift he surprised his Little One with after learning that he craves cuddle sessions every Sunday. Though cuddling has also become part of their aftercare routine, that's if Micah hasn't slipped into a peaceful slumber after the intense orgasms they exchange.

Once seated, Micah instinctively lays his head on Damon's lap, curling his legs into his chest. Damon runs his fingers through his Little One's hair while his other hand runs his fingertips up and down Micah's arm.

"Have I ever hurt you, Michelangelo? Accidentally or on purpose?"

"No," his Little One answers with no hesitation, in a quiet, sullen voice.

"Have I ever scared you? Made you fear me?"

"No."

"Then why did you wish to see how hard I would punish you?"

Damon wants to understand. He expected behaviour like this the first few months they started playing together, but now, this far into their contracted relationship, it makes no sense. Does Micah want to leave? Is he tired of following rules? Fear manifests within, but he waits for Micah to explain himself first.

"I spent my life being called a disgrace. A mistake. I was called a failure, a disappointment, a waste of space and more, all before I hit eighteen." Micah gives himself a moment before continuing. "When you've praised me, a part of me has been fighting it, believing it's all just words you say as part of the scene. But over time, I've begun to believe it. I *do* believe it…But, I suppose to be sure, I needed to do something that tested the rules you have set. To see if you still feel that way after I've disappointed you beyond actions that resulted in a punishment of writing lines or corner time."

"Do you still believe it, Michelangelo? Do you still believe that you're my good boy? That you're everything I've been searching for? Everything I've been wanting and needing after all this time?"

"Yes," Micah says with conviction.

His fingers pause from combing his Little One's hair as he leans forward and plants a kiss on his temple. "Good. Because I mean every word."

He's relieved. Today was the hardest punishment he's given Micah, and he hated every second of it. But he was embarrassed and ashamed to have his Little One behaving in such a way. He holds a reputation, and for some reason, doubt took over Micah's mind and forced them both to react in a way they didn't want.

"Your punishment today was seeing the disappointment from others, Michelangelo. Although I was upset, not once did *I* say I was disappointed in you. Remember that. Remember that at the end of the day, the *only* opinion that matters is mine. Forget about those voices. Those people. You're *my* good boy and I'm proud of you...all of you."

Micah closes his eyes, takes in a deep breath, and slowly exhales.

"I love you," Damon says with all his heart. "I never want to hurt you or see you hurting. And I'd never give you a punishment I know you couldn't handle."

Micah releases a sigh, his body calming. "Love you, too."

***

A few days after the incident, Micah sends Daddy a gift to say sorry, and thank you, to which he receives a very enthusiastic text message that has Micah blushing at work and needing to rush to the bathroom to settle himself down.

To Micah, the gift says all the things he couldn't say through words. It proves that he is taking yet another step forward into their relationship dynamic and has no desire to walk away from it, or Damon, anytime soon.

Chapter 13
Little Space Equals Safe Space

RACHEL O'ROURKE

LITTLE ONE

It's a random Wednesday and Micah is doing a stocktake of a delivery that the store received that morning. Raised voices coming from the front of the store steal his attention and stop him from continuing.

"I want a refund," Micah hears a guy around twice his age bark.

"Of course, sir, but to do that, I'm going to need you to return the book," the owner explains calmly.

"You think I still have that book? I bloody burnt it, as I should with every copy."

"Then I'm afraid I can't help you, sir."

"You'll give me my bloody money back or I'll be here with an army of parents that will—"

"What seems to be the issue?" Micah steps forward, standing tall. His shoulders are back, and he puts a hand out to check that his boss is okay.

"This hag sold my son a book of the devil," the father explains, pointing accusing fingers at the owner.

"Hmm, don't know if that's possible since we aren't a cult or a church. We're a bookstore," Micah fights back.

"Tell 'im, son. Tell 'im how I caught you reading a book that praises the homosexuals."

Suddenly, a skinny, dark-haired boy who looks no older than fifteen is thrust in front of him. At first glance, the kid reminds Micah a little of himself when he was younger, cowering under the shadow of his father's reign. But on further inspection, Micah recognises the kid. Remembers seeing him slowly shuffle toward the LGBTQIA+ romance section, looking over his shoulder as though someone was going to jump out and yell at him for even standing near the bookshelf.

He had approached the kid like he would a frightened animal, casually mentioning some of his favourite books in the genre. He got the sense that the kid was curious or closeted. Either way, the kid was seeking something from these books that he couldn't get out of life, and Micah knew a lot about that.

In the end, he offered a book that was more fluff than angst. A book that could give the kid something to daydream about, maybe even a sense of hope for the future.

"Oh, you're talking about the high school romance between Jacob and Adam."

"*You're* the one that recommended that filth to my child?"

He didn't want to out the kid. "Yeah. It's a good read. Besides, you don't have to be gay to read a gay book. Are you a vampire if you read Dracula? Are you a crazy scientist if you read Frankenstein?"

His words seem to stump and confuse the hater before him.

"Listen, don't go pushing your fagotty agenda onto my kid. One phone call from me and I could have this place shut down."

Micah runs his tongue along his bottom lip, reminding himself that this is his job, one he loves, and the golden rule is that the customer is always right.

"With all due respect, sir, our bookstore stocks a variety of genres, many of which are available for all ages, genders, races *and* sexualities."

"Ahh, I see how it is. You think you're better than me because you know a thing or two from these *books*." The father pulls his kid back, who hasn't spoken a single word, and then steps forward into Micah's personal space. "You can live in these books all you want, you pansy-ass poofter. But in the real world, guys like me are the ones that make the difference. We're the ones people listen to. *You?* You're going to die of AIDS after some guy you think loves you fucks you in an alley and spits on your face when he's done. Not even caring what your name is…" Dark, hateful eyes look down at the name tag pinned to his shirt. "…*Micah.*"

"I think it's time for you to leave," his boss's voice breaks the stare-off between him and the customer.

"Yeah," the disgruntled father agrees, "let's go, son. Who reads books these days anyway? Everything's on the fuckin' internet."

Micah watches as they leave. The son turns back around long enough to show he's sorry through the look on his face without his father catching him doing so.

When the door closes, he exhales, and then quickly walks out back before his boss can ask if he's okay.

Away from prying eyes, his body begins to shake.

What the hell is happening?

It's not like he hasn't had a disgruntled customer before. Hell, he lives for them. A chance to put assholes in their place while being friendly about it is the best feeling. But something is different this time.

His heart is racing. His palms are sweaty, and, at that moment, there is only one thing that comes to mind.

"Not feeling well, heading home for the day. I'll start early tomorrow," Micah calls out to his boss as he exits the front door, avoiding all eye contact, but knowing she won't mind his sudden departure.

As he gets in the car, he calls the only number saved in his favourites, the number currently ringing to the point where he assumes it's about to go to voicemail, even though he has *never* been sent to voicemail since day one. But then the line connects.

"Daddy?" He doesn't recognise the sound of his voice. It's panicked and high-pitched.

"Micah? What's wrong? Where are you?"

"Are you home?"

"Where are you?" Daddy ignores his question,

"Leaving work. I'm fifteen minutes away." He's more like twenty but his foot seems to be a little heavy on the accelerator.

"I'll be there. But until then, I'm going to stay on the line."

He can hear Daddy getting into his own car.

"No, no, you don't—"

"Stop!" Daddy orders.

He does.

"Don't speak. I'm right here. Just concentrate on the road and drive safely. You'll be with me soon enough."

Sixteen minutes later, Micah is leaving his keys with the valet driver. The elevator doors are being held open by the doorman for him and when Micah steps inside, Daddy is standing there waiting for him.

He crashes into Daddy's arms and the sigh of relief that falls from them both settles the frantic energy that had been building inside of him since he left work.

The doors close and they ascend towards the penthouse.

"Shhh. It's okay. Everything is okay," Daddy whispers into his ear. His hand rubs up and down the length of his back while the other grips his neck securely and protectively.

"I need it," Micah begs.

"What do you need? I'll give you anything."

He pulls back far enough to look into Daddy's eyes. "I need my teddy."

Green eyes instantly register what he's asking for and as the doors open to the penthouse floor, he's swept up in Daddy's arms—carried like a child who is sleepy or injured, or both—down the hallway towards Micah's sacred area.

Daddy stops at the door.

"You can enter, Daddy. And I'd like you to stay."

Once in the room, Daddy places him down, feet on the floor.

"Does my Little One need help changing?"

Micah nods.

It could be the energy of the room or the familiarity of the role he can slip in and out of—much like Damon can when he goes from Daddy to Dom—but as his shoes are being untied and removed from his feet, and his jeans are being unbuckled and pulled down until he is in nothing but his underwear, his mind is already in Little Space.

He holds his arms above his head as Daddy removes his shirt, replacing it with the extra-large purple one he gifted to Daddy after he misbehaved at the café. The words 'Daddy's Little One' are on the front. A declaration of the commitment to his role, and himself to Damon.

Soft, fur-like fabric is placed in his hands and Micah clings onto his teddy bear like a lifeline.

He's safe.

Unaware that his body is moving toward the loveseat, Micah crawls onto the overly large couch. The cushions perch behind him as he waits for his Daddy to sit beside him. Silently, he pulls his legs into himself, his teddy still within his grasp as he lays his head on Daddy's chest.

"It's okay, my Little One. Daddy's here."

Daddy's hand rests against his forehead and Micah exhales in relief, suddenly feeling tired. No, exhausted. Like he's been awake for seventy-two hours, fighting against every monster he has ever read about, along with the demons he slayed while growing up.

"Rest, Michelangelo. Everything will be okay."

***

"I don't understand what happened. What he said, it was nothing new," Micah questions after relaying the altercation that led Micah to him midweek, outside of their play schedule.

They are still cuddling on the loveseat, though when Micah wakes up, Damon is watching a movie on the TV, subtitles on with the sound muted so as not to disturb his Little One. He had even placed a weighted blanket on top to help settle Micah's anxiety, allowing him to sleep more peacefully.

"I think the answer is quite simple, Michelangelo." Damon's thumb gently caresses his Little One's cheek. "Your time in Little Space has connected you to your younger self in a way that now causes you to react emotionally when degrading things are said to you."

"So, being a Little has made me weak?"

"Oh, my precious boy, no. Quit the opposite. Being a Little has made you stronger."

"I don't see how being on the verge of tears at my job is being strong."

"The disgruntled customer isn't what upset you. The homophobic words and the way he belittled you, forcing you to feel less superior to him is what caused it."

"Still waiting for the part that makes me stronger…"

"You're stronger because you know now that none of it is real. In the past, those words would have echoed in your mind for the remainder of the day, alongside your father's, and all you would have done is brushed them off because it was nothing you hadn't been called before. You probably would have had a few drinks after work, or even perhaps visited the club to lose yourself in a scene. Avoidance through self-destruction."

Damon doesn't miss the small hint of guilt and recognition on Micah's face when he mentions self-destruction.

"But now, you have learnt to accept that none of those things are *you*. They never were and they never will be. Had you been able to react like a child does while growing up, after your father said such vile things to you, your body would have felt much like it has today. So yes, Michelangelo, to me, this proves how much stronger you are since connecting with your Little. Instead of self-destructing, you went to a safe space. You came back to your room where you could feel all these emotions and process them the way a child would learn to while growing up."

He couldn't be prouder of the way Micah sought him out and told him that he needed to be in his room, his place to feel safe.

"Who you are, your sexuality and your desires, does not make you a freak. Being emotional does not make you weak. And being able to stay calm, while someone tries to undermine you by being boisterous, homophobic and rude already shows that you're a better person than they are."

Like stepping into Little Space, this, too, may be something that Micah will need to sit with to fully understand.

"It's okay," Damon speaks his thoughts, "this, too, is new. But I promise it will eventually make sense."

They're sitting at the dining table eating the comfort food Damon ordered, knowing the greasy burgers would help. Micah drags a french fry through a puddle of ketchup, and Damon loves how domestic the whole situation feels.

"Damon." Micah uses his name, making alarm bells go off inside his head.

"If what you said is true, about my connection through Little Space or whatever…does that mean this is over?"

Damon makes eye contact with Micah before sitting back in his chair. He keeps his face neutral, though he suspects this is the beginning of the end.

"Is that what you think?" Damon asks.

Micah shrugs. "We started this so you could help me connect. Help me get closure. Help me learn how to grow in life through Little Space. So, I mean…" The younger man's words float away.

"Do you remember what I told you on the phone before we met up?" he questions.

That was almost a year ago, but Micah's silence is a sufficient answer.

"I said you're in control. You have been every day since. So, my question is, *do you* want this to be over?" He pauses. "Do you want to rip up our contract?"

Chapter 14

Eternity

RACHEL O'ROURKE

After the incident at work and the way that Damon lovingly took care of him, Micah decides that he no longer wants a contract. He no longer wants a piece of paper to determine the rules of his relationship with Damon.

"I don't want this anymore," Micah confesses. A flicker of remorse breaks out across Damon's face, but he covers it well.

"Understood. I'll get the contract."

Micah thinks that this is it. That Damon is happy for them to part ways. That's until he notices the dejection on Damon's face. With the confidence Micah has learnt to possess over the months he's shared with Damon, he knows it's now or never to use his voice and be true to himself.

"What I want," his words stop Damon as he goes to stand, "is to be your everything."

Micah's heart begins to race. His mouth is dry, but he holds on to the confidence he has built up over the last year to help him explain what he wants.

"I want to come home to Damon Stone every day of the week, not just weekends. I want Dom Daddy to fuck my brains out and make love to me. I want to be able to escape into Little Space whenever I need to break away and have Daddy take care of me when I do." His voice trembles but he keeps going. "I want to be seen standing beside Damon and have the world know he's off limits because he's mine and I love him. I. Love. Him…in every version of the word."

"You know," Damon begins. "I was starting to worry that I might have had to end our contract. That I'd have to step in and be the one to enforce that it's time to put a stop to it all."

That dreaded fear slowly creeps back up to the surface.

"Because," Damon stands, slowly making his way around the table, "I wasn't sure how much longer I could pretend that you don't mean more to me than just a name on a piece of paper."

Micah doesn't have time to bask in the relief before Damon has him enveloped in his arms. Their kiss is passionate, and desperate, as though it is going to be their last. But Micah knows it's the first of the many to come.

Michelangelo Sampson is now the boyfriend, lover, partner *and* Submissive of one Damon Stone. It's funny how he openly admits this now, that he is a Submissive. When he first stepped into this world, he refused to believe he would submit, because he didn't see himself as being able to follow rules and orders. But what he has come to learn is that he is *Damon's* Submissive, not *a* Submissive. And it's through his submission to Damon that he has connected with his strength, confidence and assertiveness that allows him to stand up and be himself in a way he didn't know was possible.

They see each other not only on the weekend but also during the week when they go on dates that involve movies, dinners, games of pool at the bar, and trips to bookstores all over the city. Micah spends hours looking at first editions and rare finds from authors that only published one book, which was written ahead of its time.

They hold hands in public and fight over who pays for what, though most of the time, Damon wins. They argue. Micah raises his voice, swears and storms out of the room, only to eventually settle down and walk back so he can calmly talk to Damon about why he reacted so strongly.

What Micah has found in Damon is a person who accepts him for who he is: an opinionated homosexual who is strong, independent, and craves attention when he wants his mind to shut off. He loves to be fucked within an inch of his life and enjoys being spanked until his ass matches the colour of a ripened tomato. He is someone who will reach for his teddy, slip on an overly baggy T-shirt and spend hours in his room when he needs to disconnect from the world and connect with himself.

Damon is his Daddy, but sometimes, he's just Damon. What they admitted that day when he asked Damon to rip up the contract was that they no longer wanted three days a week together. They had both been wanting more, too scared to address it with the other. They wanted every second of every minute with no rules on how to treat each other, they just wanted to be together.

That doesn't mean he is going back to eating like he's fifteen years old. The change in his lifestyle continues as he takes the lessons learnt and applies them to their romantic relationship. There are still rules for when they are in a scene, for the times Daddy comes out, remembering how Damon still needs that twenty-four-seven lifestyle to feel grounded. Their dynamic hasn't changed too drastically from what it was before. Though now, he might come home from a long day at work and find Damon cooking for him in his overly cramped kitchen because he has a key to his apartment, something that had been long overdue.

Micah stands by Damon's side and is introduced as his partner when Damon has important business meetings. He awakens anytime between Monday to Sunday being held tight, a reminder that he is always going to be cared for and safe.

***

The adjustment hadn't taken long. Damon had wanted to show the world that Micah was his since the day he signed the contract. Now, he can do it knowing that the man he loves is standing beside him because he wants to, not because he has to. What took time was remembering that a slither of control had to be given back to Micah. Whether it be Micah paying for a meal, the decision to sleep over at his small studio apartment over Damon's well-kept penthouse, or simply what movie they were going to watch that night. Micah understands the man he is and therefore knows when to push back and when to accept defeat.

A few months into their newly formed relationship, he once again brings up the idea of Micah coming with him to the club. The same club they met at many months ago.

"Yeah, I'm ready," Micah clarifies.

"Ready?"

"You're going to think it's stupid but, I kind of didn't feel confident enough to be seen in public as your Sub."

Micah is right, that does sound stupid, but Damon hears him out.

"I just wanted to be perfect for you. I wanted to know exactly what to do and how to act. You're like royalty in that world. Everyone wants to be with you or be like you."

"Oh, baby." He pulls Micah into his arms, removing the space between them on the couch. "You forget that the rules are what we make them. If we stepped into the club and I told you I wanted you to be a brat so I could tame you in front of everyone, then that's what we would have done. No one would have walked away saying how disobedient you were, they would have walked away saying how well you respond to discipline." Perhaps this is one element he failed to explain properly.

"BDSM clubs were originally built so people had a space they could go to that helped them find others with their kind of interests. This was before Grindr and Fetlife and whatever else is out there. Then they stopped being just a place to meet someone and became a place to play in public, for those that like to watch, or be seen, or learn."

"In other words…no one there is perfect."

"Exactly. Look at the day we met to who you are now. You were still attending the club scenes back then, and yet you know so much more now. Understand it better, too."

"You're right. I never thought of it like that."

"No rush. The decision to return is up to you."

★★★

Attending the clubs as a Submissive who is owned has its own kind of power. Micah can still recall what it was like to walk in and find someone to play with, needing a different kind of confidence when asking others for what he wanted. Now, when he walks into the club where he first met Damon, the same club that is connected to another part of himself, an older version that he only vaguely recognises; he knows that *he is loved* by the man who owns him, who plays with him, and who has collared him and claimed him to forever be his.

Exactly one year after their contract is destroyed, Daddy presents him with an eternity collar, a symbol he recalls being the most serious when it comes to collars. As he reaches out and lays his fingers on the thin, black titanium ring, he notices there is no clasp to secure it around his neck.

"There is a small screw that will allow it to open and lock," Daddy explains. "If you wish, you can wear it twenty-four seven. It's lightweight so you can sleep in it, and it won't tarnish from water, not even from a pool or the ocean." Daddy begins to use the small screwdriver to remove the tiniest screw he has ever seen, allowing the collar to open much like handcuffs.

"Or you can choose to wear it only when we go out, whether that be dinner or to the clubs. The choice is yours, Michelangelo. Whether you choose to wear it permanently or only for occasions, I'll still know that you'll forever be mine."

He holds the collar, his hands shaking as he takes in the significance of Daddy's gesture. He has seen many Submissives throughout the year wearing various collars, though never one as sleek and elegant as the one in his grasp.

He decides that if he is going to do this, he might as well be his true self while he does. "If this collar can come off, then what makes you think it's forever?"

That's when he looks up and sees Daddy holding a white gold wedding band with the eternity symbol engraved on the top, the letters D and M within each circle.

"Because although you're not always my Submissive, I'd like for you to always be my husband."

Three months later, in an intimate collaring ceremony, he and Damon exchange promises and vows as Daddy places the collar around his neck while they say 'I do' through the exchange of wedding rings. They are bound together through every version of themselves. Damon and Micah, partners and lovers, Daddy and Little One, Dominate and Submissive.

Micah now proudly walks beside his Daddy, not behind him, because to Damon, they are equals. He's proud of the few glances he gets as people stare at his collar and whisper how he is the one Damon Stone chose to spend forever with. How he is the one who could fulfil Damon's Dominant persona.

Daddy takes a seat on the large, rounded couch that is now situated in the corner of the club where he knows to sit like a prized possession. He always sits to the side, half on his Daddy's lap, and half on the soft couch, legs stretched out over his Daddy's thighs, who likes to wrap a hand over his ankle and squeeze it throughout the night. This way, Damon is still seen as the one in charge, but his position shows that Daddy doesn't view him as anything less than his other half. The rounded couch has been moved away from where it sat that first night he lay across Daddy's lap, taking the spanking that sparked the fire between them. Its relocation was made mostly for privacy, but also so Damon can overlook everything that he owns.

It didn't take long for word to get out that Damon Stone has a life partner. A very well-behaved one at that, which created an opportunity for Damon to invest in the club he had been pursuing for years, and the chance to buy up enough shares to own more than fifty per cent, making Damon the new owner.

Micah leans into Daddy, watching the scenes of others play out before them. They have three rules when attending the clubs. The first: they can both look, but never touch. It's a rule that seems futile since neither of them ever wants anyone but each other. They don't believe in sharing. Damon is a possessive man and every bone in Micah's body is made up of jealousy. Regardless, it's safer to state the rules, than simply assume them.

The second rule: they play in private. Damon's clubs have a 'no sex in public' policy, the back rooms reserved for such an activity, which also requires a membership for patrons to partake in. However, the open space can be used for all other scenes that wish to be played out. Although he had dropped his pants multiple times for some stranger to flog and paddle, his Daddy now wishes to keep that part of him to himself. In Daddy's words, Micah's vulnerability when they play is something Daddy doesn't wish for others to see. Daddy wants him to be able to sink into the sensation in a quiet, relaxed atmosphere, where his husband can care for and slowly nurture him back from the blankness of his mind.

The third rule: Daddy is in charge. From the second they step foot into the club, Daddy does everything for him. He decides what Micah eats, what he drinks, where he sits, and what he wears. It's all Daddy, and Micah loves every fucking second of it.

This is his life now, nuzzling into the broad-shoulder alpha-like male who eyed him from across the room for weeks before making a move. He has plans to buy out the bookstore so his boss can retire early, thanks to Damon and his never-ending desire to spend any amount of money to make him happy. He has plans to turn it into an indie author bookstore like he had always dreamed; the focus being on LGBTQIA+ authors and books.

He knows how he got to where he is today. He remembers every moment with his parents up until the day he took his first spanking.

What he also knows is that everybody has their own kinks. They have them for different pleasures and they partake in them for various reasons, all getting a particular release from said kinks. He has no shame in liking what he likes. He is not embarrassed by the things he does in and out of the bedroom. He is a soon-to-be twenty-seven-year-old who calls a thirty-seven-year-old Daddy. Who watches Disney movies while colouring in, who sometimes sleeps with a teddy bear while other times needs his prostate milked to get a good night's rest.

He is Micah Sampson-Stone. A 'little' homosexual. And he couldn't be happier.